Endorsements

"It has been said, 'Home is where the heart is.' In her new book, *Rooms of Her Heart*, Paulette Phillips leads us on a home tour, using metaphors to illustrate issues at the core of a woman's heart. She invites you to fling open the door of your heart and allow the truth of God's Word to expose and heal any difficult areas of pain."

—Brenda J. Kilpatrick
Pastor's Wife, Brownsville Assembly of God
Founder of Awake Deborah Ministries

"In every room of our hearts, Paulette gently rubs the healing balm of Christ into the sensitive areas of our lives. As a result, we as women of God are healed, delivered and restored by the power of God."

—Joni T. Lamb
Daystar Television Network

"In this neat and fitting house that Paulette Phillips has constructed, she encourages us to examine our lives room by room and allows God to uncover, reveal and expose the things that would hinder and stunt our growth as His obedient children. This easy-to-read, very pointed and inspiring book helps you deal with emotional pain, frustration and discouragement. It will be a blessing to those who need to do some personal introspection."

—Judy Jacobs-Tuttle
International Speaker and Vocalist

"Paulette Phillips is a woman of God who has fulfilled many roles during her years of ministry. The 'rooms of her heart' have experienced inspection and rearranging many times. She now steps forward, qualified to equip women to place their lives in the Master's hands. In *Rooms of Her Heart*, women will find strength to face the everyday challenges that life brings. The key to living in victory is a change in mind-set. This book offers practical keys to living free! Thanks, Paulette, for sharing the 'rooms of your heart' with us."

—*Reita Ball, Copastor*
Metropolitan Tabernacle
Chattanooga, Tennessee

"People are naturally drawn to Paulette Phillips because of her passion for life and her deep love of God. She greets each day with a creative enthusiasm that is contagious! As an interior designer, I admire her talents for design and decorating and respect her values in creating a God-centered home. In *Rooms of Her Heart*, Paulette teaches the principles of Spirit-filled living. My life has been made richer by knowing her not only as a friend, but also as a dear soul-sister in Christ."

—*Patti A. Wilde*
Designer and Owner
Ethan Allen Gallaries
Knoxville, Tennessee

"As I began to read *Rooms of Her Heart*, I felt as though Paulette Phillips was walking through the rooms of *my* heart and writing directly to me! Dealing with current issues with which we all identify, she shines the revealing light of Scripture on our daily walk and relationships with God and the people with whom we interact. Paulette has the gift of discernment, sharing practical understandings and spiritual wisdom from her own large 'cupboard' of real-life happenings. In this day of mixed signals and garbled values, this book makes a valuable contribution to clearer vision of what we can become if only we will live out our Savior's unique intentions for each of us."

—*Minette Drumwright Pratt*
Speaker and Writer

"Paulette Baker Phillips is a woman of many gifts. For more than 20 years she taught writing along with her specialty, British literature. A few years ago, God summoned her dramatically and suddenly from the classroom to the pulpit!

As a part of her role as director of women's ministries, she teaches 'The Haven Bible Study' every Tuesday at 10 a.m. Each week the room is filled with women who are hungry for the Word. As her pastor (and husband), I hear about everything sooner or later. A particular series called "Rooms of Her Heart" was having a powerful impact. At a 2003 Media Partner Weekend, Paulette spoke on "The Hallway of Transition." Soon after, I had her share that message on a Sunday with our entire church.

This book contains that message and others. The teacher has become the writer! This book has an anointing that will liberate men and women alike. It may well be the best book you will read this year! I am proud of Paulette and this milestone in her life."

—*Dr. Ron M. Phillips*
Pastor's study ABBA's House

"In *Rooms of Her Heart*, Paulette Phillips presents the rooms of a home as a metaphor to address the everyday issues of a woman's heart. You will find instruction and healing from God's Word through this powerful book. You will also discover that as you apply God's Word, the rooms of your heart can be filled with precious and pleasant riches. Your life will be changed through the ministry of Paulette."

—Pastor Paula White
Without Walls International Church

"In her book, *Rooms of Her Heart*, Paulette opens the door for all of us to tour our own 'heart house.' With the Holy Spirit as our guide, we are given the opportunity to inspect rooms we frequently visit and unlock the doors to rooms that have been closed away for years. She graciously calls us to a spiritual housecleaning that leaves us clean and free of the clutter that keeps us afraid to go out and ashamed to let others in. So open the door and come on in . . . it's time to get started."

—Karen Wheaton
Karen Wheaton Ministries

ROOMS of Her HEART

Karen,

Blessings

Paulette Phillips

PAULETTE BAKER PHILLIPS

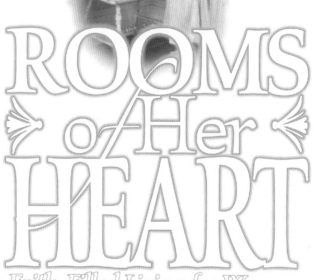

ROOMS of Her HEART

Faith-Filled Living for Women

Pathway
PRESS

Book Editor: Wanda Griffith
Editorial Assistant: Tammy Hatfield
Copy Editors: Esther Metaxas
Cresta Shawver

Library of Congress Catalog Card Number: 2003113237
ISBN: 0-87148-135-9
Copyright © 2003 by Pathway Press
Cleveland, Tennessee 37311
All Rights Reserved
Printed in the United States of America

Dedication

To my dear husband, Ron: Next to the Lord, you are my treasured friend. You have been my cheerleader throughout this project and, at times, pushed me to complete it. Thank you for mentoring me in the faith and for loving me unconditionally. You have impacted my life greatly and I love you.

To my children and grandchildren:

> Kelli Phillips Logue and Kevin Logue and my grandsons Ethan, Owen and Collin Logue.

> Heather Phillips Wooten and Cain Wooten and my grandson Maxwell Wooten and granddaughter Ava Elisabeth Wooten.

> Kelly Nicole and Ronnie Phillips Jr. and my grandson Ronnie Phillips III (Trey).

You fill my life with excitement, joy and fulfillment in who you are and what you are doing with your beautiful lives. I love you all.

To my parents, Bill and Pauline Baker: You have been a profound influence on my life, providing a rock of strength and a compass for my way. Thank you for believing in me. I am honored to be your daughter. I love you.

Table of Contents

Acknowledgments

I offer sincere appreciation to . . .

The women and leadership and prayer group of the Haven Bible Study who pray for me and encourage me weekly as we study God's Word. Also to the family of Central Baptist Church. Thanks for your unfailing love and support through more than two decades.

The faithful friends, editors and encouragers at Central Church: Carolyn Sutton, Margy Barber, Rae Bond and Susan Foster. Also thanks to the great editing staff at Pathway Press: Wanda Griffith, Tammy Hatfield, Esther Metaxas and Cresta Shawver.

Our Lord and Savior Jesus Christ is the answer to my needs and the source of my contentment. I am thankful that He came to give me life and give it more abundantly. He promised us that out of our hearts would flow rivers of living water (John 7:38). We don't have to allow our hearts to be troubled if we believe on Christ. May this work bring honor to Him.

Introduction

There it was—the most beautiful house I had ever seen. Every room was what I had dreamed of. It was stylish and spacious, with built-in extras featured in every room. The golf course in the back added to its charm. Of course, as a newlywed, I knew the dream was far beyond the reach of our meager budget. But it was fun to tour the house and imagine what it would be like to set up housekeeping there!

Most women will never have the house of their dreams—but they can have the life of their dreams! My goal in this book is to accompany you on a tour of another house—the house of your life—and see what a fulfilling life you can live as a woman.

Maybe you are young and still under construction. Maybe you are older and feel your life desperately needs remodeling. No matter where you are in life's journey, you can build your life room-by-room, and in the process, understand that you are unique, beautiful and valuable.

Women share so many wonderful things: ambitions, home building, motherhood, careers, friendships, relationships, talents, fashion, conscience and dedication. Have you ever noticed that many women can sit down with a stranger and chat for hours about anything and not miss a breath?

Women have passion for many things. Our homes are at the core of our existence whether it is a dorm room, an efficiency apartment, a sprawling ranch, a condominium, a houseboat or a retirement village. In our homes, we exhibit style, beauty, charm and comfort. But we continue decorating and remodeling, and we never seem to finish. The catalog companies know this. That's why we receive an endless stream of them daily in our mailboxes!

Women are free to change their minds about anything, especially decorating and remodeling! We want to change the carpet, the paint, the furniture, the style and the arrangement, so our homes are always a work in progress. In the same way spiritually, we are also a work in progress as individual, creative, maturing women of faith.

Our homes will never be perfect, but neither will we. However, God is always perfect. He is faithful, strong and true. We may not be right, but God is.

Throughout this book, I use the rooms of your home as metaphors to illustrate issues at the core of a woman's heart. As you read about loneliness, sexual intimacy, prayer, organization, hospitality, transition, parenting, salvation or hidden sins, I hope you will fling open the door of your heart and allow the truth of God's Word to expose and heal any difficult areas of pain. Maybe not every room discussed here will expose a need in your heart, but some will definitely touch a nerve. As you read this book and work through the study questions, allow the promises of God to reside in your heart so you will not sin against Him (Psalm 119:11).

Women are generally sensitive souls. We have needs and want quick, pat answers. We cry so hard and lose hope. We work jobs, feed our families, do laundry, meet deadlines, and fuss about our hair and gaining weight. We brag on our babies and grieve over our teenagers. We love the good times and hate the bad. Sometimes we can't get enough of God, and other times we blame Him for our situation.

It is my prayer that the truths in this book will be a foundational stone—a place where women can have powerful encounters that bring about change in their lives; a place to lay down all the painful baggage that hinders them from becoming completely free and experiencing the greatness of God in extraordinary ways.

—Paulette B. Phillips

"Sanctify the Lord God in your hearts: and be
ready always to give an answer to every man
that asketh you a reason of the hope that is in you
with meekness and fear"
(1 Peter 3:15, KJV).

I am a part of all that I have met;
Yet all experience is an arch wherethrough
Gleams that untraveled world whose margin fades
For ever and for ever when I move.
How dull it is to pause, to make an end,
To rust unburnished, not to shine in use!
—Alfred Lord Tennyson,
Ulysses, Lines 18-23

1

The Foyer of New Beginnings

Can you identify with emotions of dissatisfaction, frustration, incompleteness, unhappiness, powerlessness or unsettledness? Have these words accurately described you at some juncture in your life?

I must confess that as a young pastor's wife, I lived with all of that insecurity. To admit this in religious circles meant to reveal that my life was not perfect, my relationships were not complete, and my well-being was fragile. After all, religious people should have all the answers; they should not be consumed with unanswered questions—or so I thought!

My unhappiness was not just in one particular area of my life, but with my life in general. I suffered silently because I feared the disapproval of those whose opinions I valued. I needed a new beginning in my life, a new direction. I needed a door of hope.

Building a First Impression
When visitors enter your home, they usually step into

your foyer. This area just inside the front door is generally the first impression a visitor has of your home, and a first impression is usually a lasting impression. Just as the entryway provides the first glimpse of a house, your heart is the open door to who you are.

Early in my life, I carefully decorated the foyer of my life the way I thought others should see it. Born into a Christian family, I had attended church since I was an infant. At 10 years of age, at the end of a sermon, I walked down to the front of the Baptist church and genuinely desired to be saved.

I was baptized, and for years I believed that I was a Christian. Years later, I realized that all that time, I was working my way to God. I did not consciously believe in a salvation by works, but that is exactly what I was doing. At a subconscious level, I learned how to please my parents, to do my work at school, to achieve, to be the teacher's pet, and to get accolades and success, and erroneously, I thought I could also impress God.

I did all the right things and played by the rules. I tried so hard to be a Christian, which included being a part of everything that went on at church—from classes, Girl's Auxiliary, Acteens, Sunday school, Training Union and Scripture memorization.

By age 15, I was on the church payroll, directing three choirs and playing the piano in services. As a church leader and president of our youth group, I was the perfect overachiever, but the front foyer of my life was deceptive: I was not saved! I had not yet realized that my righteous acts were like filthy rags before God.

Early in life, I put a veil over the foyer of my life.

People did not get to know the real me. I regret to say that the first impression others had of me was superficial and shallow. The door of my heart was closed to God and His ways. Inside, I was empty and sterile, with only an echo of my own selfish cries. There was no room in the foyer of my life for anyone else.

Early in life, I put a veil over the foyer of my life. People did not get to know the real me.

Believing there was a destiny in my life, I attended Samford University to work on a major in music and education. While a student, I married the man of my dreams, Ron Phillips, whom I had known most of my life. I strongly believed we would be partners in Christian ministry. But then my life became a nightmare.

The Christian ministry became my nightmare. My biggest sin was the sin of pride. I wanted what I wanted, the way I wanted it, when I wanted it, how I wanted it, and all I wanted. I was unhappy. Nothing I did brought me satisfaction. In the small church my husband pastored, I played the piano, taught preschoolers, worked with teenagers, and was still unfulfilled. I did not know what to do. Life for me was miserable.

I was 21 years old and felt tired, worn out and just about at the end of myself. I began to think, *O God, I may have made a terrible mistake marrying a minister!* I remember crying out, "I cannot do this any longer." My pride and determination had always kept me going. In most situations, I was able to pull myself up by my own bootstraps. But although I prayed and read my Bible, I had never given God complete control of my thoughts, my ambitions, my life, my future, my heart, soul, mind and spirit. I had memorized chapters of Scripture and knew the plan of salvation, but I was "of all men most miserable" (1 Corinthians 15:19, KJV). In my life I had a form of godliness, but I was denied the power of true godliness.

A Door of Hope

During the summer of 1969, Ron and I worked as counselors at a youth camp in Cook Springs, Alabama. No way did I want to be there, but it was one of those situations I could not get out of gracefully. The commute to and from Samford University gave me a little reprieve each day.

On Wednesday night of that camp week, after our friend Dudley Hall preached, my husband and I walked off alone to talk. I told him frankly that I was at the end of my rope. Everywhere I turned seemed to be a dead-end street, and I just couldn't go on. I was so unhappy. What had gone wrong with the perfect life I had planned? "It is just too hard to be a Christian," I said.

My dear preacher husband immediately saw my need. He said, "Honey, will you please go over the Romans road to heaven with me one more time?" After we read Romans 3:23—that "all have sinned and fall short of the glory of God"—I prayed and said, "Lord, I know I am a sinner, and I know that God's Son, Jesus, died for my sins. I know that 'the wages of sin is death, but the gift of God is eternal life in Christ Jesus our Lord'" (6:23).

I continued to pray: "Please, Lord, forgive me of my sins, come into my life and save me. Be the Lord of my life and I will love You, worship You and serve You with my life." I prayed, "God, if You can do anything for me, save me and give me the abundant life of the New Testament."

God seemed to say, "Paulette, this is what I have been waiting for all this time. You cannot save yourself, and your righteous works are like filthy rags (Isaiah 64:6). I died for you because I love you." I had finally realized that salvation has nothing to do with my works—it is all about what He can do.

I no longer had simply a "head knowledge" of Christianity; I had a new heart relationship with the God of the universe.

That warm summer night, God very quietly and gloriously forgave my sins (especially my pride), and became my Lord and Savior. I no longer had simply a "head knowledge" of Christianity; I had a new heart relationship with the God of the universe. Since that night, I have never doubted my salvation. His love and forgiveness are free to all who ask and receive Him.

First Steps Into a New Foyer

Thank God, my 22-year-old pastor husband was not ashamed of me or embarrassed by my decision. He told me I needed "believer's baptism." My pride briefly reared its head again, because the thought of being baptized in front of the church people we pastored was embarrassing! I thought this could be just between God and me. My husband decreed that on Sunday morning, I would tell our congregation what had happened to me, and he would baptize me on Sunday night. I knew that had to happen, for Romans 10:9 states that we should "confess with [our] mouth the Lord Jesus."

Sleep did not come easily between Wednesday night and Sunday morning for fear the people would laugh at me—a preacher's wife who had never really been a believer! I was afraid they would mock me or be ashamed of me. I was even fearful that my husband might be fired from his position as pastor.

I cared too much what people might think. The Enemy tried to make me feel ashamed for having lived a lie before the church. But I was reminded of these scriptures:

God demonstrates His own love toward us, in that while we were still sinners, Christ died for us (Romans 5:8).

There is therefore now no condemnation . . . in Christ Jesus (8:1).

Although I was afraid, God gave me the strength to give my testimony. Hallelujah, none of my fears materialized! The fears were lies from the Enemy. Our church family embraced me, loved me, encouraged me and blessed me. One dear deacon's wife and friend twice my age came to the altar at the end of service and told the church that my testimony of struggle was the same as hers, and she wanted to give Christ control of her life. Every time I give this testimony, God ministers salvation to someone.

Examine Your Heart

John 10:9 says of Jesus, "I am the door. If anyone enters, he will be saved." Jesus Christ was the door of a new beginning for me. He was the open door to a new and glorious life. This was the beginning of a marvelous journey that continues and grows even today.

The doorway to your heart is Christ. Others first see His presence in the foyer of your heart. When He is there, He controls your heart and all the rooms of your house. Through the door of Christ, we are forever changed. God may change what you like and what you don't like. He may change your friends, career, mentors, speech and witness just as He did mine. But Jesus promised that His yoke is easy and His burden is light (Matthew 11:30).

Perhaps you need a new beginning in your life. You can begin again with the new birth of Christ! Salvation means being rescued from jeopardy. It means you can be forgiven and can live life eternally with Him.

God has been in the saving business for a long time. In the Old Testament . . .

 ᛦ Israel was saved from slavery in Egypt.

 ᛦ Jonah, a rebellious and stubborn preacher, was saved from the fish's belly.

 ᛦ Ruth, a foreigner from Moab who had suffered loss

and had nothing to call her own, was blessed by God and placed in the lineage of Christ.

When we accept Christ, we are rescued from sin and its consequences. We are saved from a life of sin (Romans 6:21). We are saved from a life of fear (8:15). We are saved from eternal death (6:23).

Matthew 7:7 says, "Seek, and you will find; knock, and it will be opened to you." This means to ask and God will give to you. What are you in need of as you knock? Is it forgiveness, salvation, direction, provisions or guidance? Knock, ask, and you shall have!

Jesus took our sins on Himself on the cross and cast them as far as the east is from the west, because He is the resurrection and the life.

Forgiven, Forgotten

In the great allegory *Pilgrim's Progress,* John Bunyan tells the story of Christian, who represents mankind, as he travels to the Celestial City (heaven) with a heavy load (sin) on his back. When Christian reached the Cross, the burden dropped off his back, tumbled and fell in the Tomb, and was never seen again. This is a beautiful picture of salvation!

Jesus took our sins on Himself on the cross and cast them as far as the east is from the west, because He is the resurrection and the life. He remembers our sin no more. Once we have asked for and received Christ's salvation, we are no longer sinners, for God has removed, forgiven and forgotten all our confessed sins. When we feel guilty and consumed by past faults, God does not know what we are talking about or thinking about, because when God forgives, He also forgets. When you remember your sin, know that the Enemy has reminded you of it.

We serve a God of new beginnings. Revelation 3:20 states that Jesus said of Himself, "Behold, I stand at the door and knock. If anyone hears My voice and opens the door, I will come in to him and dine with him, and he with Me." Christ wants to come through the door of your heart into the foyer to give you a new beginning—a new start and a new heart. Open the door of your heart today to a God who loves you! It takes only a simple, childlike trust, but it brings liberation when you give Christ the open door to your life!

Review Questions

1. The door, a vehicle for entering or leaving, is an essential part of a house. Scripture refers to a door of hope many times. Look up these passages and reflect on the hope God extended and promised:

   ꙮ Hosea 2:15 mentions the Valley of Achor, which is the sin of Achan; in place of that sin, one can now have a door of hope. Can you remember a sin that God has taken away and given you the door of hope?

   ꙮ Matthew 7:7 is a reminder to keep knocking. Be relentless. Don't stop asking!

   ꙮ Revelation 3:7, 8, 20 talks about the door Jesus has set before us. What do you need to say "yes" to Him about today?

   ꙮ John 10:9 describes the door to Christ. Think back to the moment of your salvation.

2. Define the word *salvation*:_____

3. In each of the following scriptures, people were rescued from what?

   Exodus 15:2

   Psalm 116:6

Jonah 2:9

Romans 5:9

Romans 6:14, 18

Romans 6:21, 23

Romans 8:15

1 Thessalonians 1:10

4. Review your own salvation experience and tell someone soon.

"Blessed be the Lord,
Because He has heard the voice of my supplications!
The Lord is my strength and my shield;
My heart trusted in Him, and I am helped;
Therefore my heart greatly rejoices,
And with my song I will praise Him"
(Psalm 28:6, 7).

2

The Living Room of Prayer

When I was a girl growing up in the 1960s, the living room of our home was decorated with beautiful furniture. It was untouched, because it had a white sofa, lovely shag carpeting and a piano. There was no television, and we couldn't play in this room because it was reserved for company and conversation! It was *always* clean.

I had a unique attachment to the room, however. I felt as if this room belonged to me because I went there every day to practice the piano. As the oldest of six children, I enjoyed the quiet solitude of this special room.

Today our living rooms are much more functional. We live, work and play in them. Whether we label this room the great room, the living room, the bonus room, the keeping room, the library or the music room—activity and action fill the space. But when the activity of the day is absent, what better use of this room than to use it as a place of prayer!

A Time to Pray

Christians know prayer should be a daily exercise, but as a busy woman, you may ask, "When can I pray? My intentions are good, but the children, the jobs, the telephone and the errands consume my hours. When the day comes to a close, I realize I've missed my prayer time once again!"

Jesus knew the toil of a busy life. Mark 1:35 says of our Lord, "Now in the morning, having risen a long while before daylight, He . . . departed to a solitary place; and there He prayed." In spite of the intense mission and constant demands on His time, Jesus prayed before every decision or event in His life. He prayed prior to calling the 12 disciples, before performing miracles, before healing the sick, before feeding the thousands, before raising Lazarus from the dead, before His trial and during His crucifixion. Often He left crowds standing, awaiting His ministry, so He could steal away to a solitary place. If it was imperative for Jesus to pray to the Father, how much more should we pray?

Prayer must be a priority. We know as women that the thing that screams loudest in our lives is what gets our attention. However, you can carve out a portion of every day to communicate with God. If you are a morning person, as I am, you can enjoy a steaming cup of coffee and spend your quiet time with God as the sun rises. Your peak time may be during lunch, after an afternoon jog or late evening when the rest of the household is sleeping.

Lessons in Prayer

You may say, "Once I find the time, how do I get started?" This is an age-old question—one the disciples asked our Lord when they said, "Teach us to pray." In response, Jesus gave them the Lord's Prayer: "Our Father in heaven . . ." (Matthew 6:9-13).

How do you start to pray? You just do it. There is no wrong way to pray. Prayer is simply speaking with God and inviting Him to work in your life. How amazing it is to talk to the God of the universe and have the Father God listen and answer us with love, change and miracles! It is not what we say that impresses God, because He already knows all we need before we ask Him. He is simply interested in hearing us come to Him in praise, worship, thanksgiving and confession of our sins.

Prayer is not getting our will to God, but it is about getting God's will to us.

God has commanded us to pray. Scripture says that we "alway ought to pray and not lost heart" (Luke 18:1). We should pray in good times or bad times, in sunshine or storms, in quiet seasons or turbulent roars, in happy times or sorrowful days. Our God is interested in all things pertaining to us, His children.

As we sit in the living room of prayer, we can have the assurance that God answers prayer. He answers the mental, the emotional, the practical, the financial, the physical and the spiritual needs! His mandate is that we pray without ceasing and that we always be in an attitude of prayer. Prayer is not getting *our* will to God, but it is about getting God's will to us. God may not change your husband whom you are praying for, or immediately fix your wayward child—but He will change YOU as you pray.

Praise

When we approach God in prayer, words of praise should come out of our mouths first. Praise is not just an upbeat song in church—praise is bragging on God! In the same way we compliment our friends and family for their actions and kindness toward us, praise is complimenting God on what He has done. Praise allows us to acknowledge how faithful God has been.

What has He done for you? Has God answered prayers about your family, husband, children, health, finances, future, jobs, difficult relationships, and your hopes and dreams? Do you praise God for a home, for life itself, for America, for food, and for finances? God cares about each of us individually! Psalm 84:11 states: "No good thing will He withhold from those who walk uprightly."

The Greek philosopher Aristotle said, "We are what we repeatedly do." When we repeatedly pray, we become people of prayer and intercession. When we praise, we brag on God and what He does for us.

Worship

To have an intimate relationship with God, we must worship Him. In our prayer time, our worship celebrates *who God is*. This is different from praise. Worship is literally celebrating the character of God. We rejoice that He is merciful, holy, righteous, powerful, sovereign, forgiving and loving. In our time of private worship, we can lift Him up and magnify, or focus, on God.

Worship is literally celebrating the character of God.

The amazing change that takes place during our worship is that God begins to lift us up as well! We receive the assurance in prayer that we are . . .

- ♥ A favored child

- ♥ The apple of His eye

- ♥ An ambassador for Him

- ♥ Powerful and blessed

- ♥ Righteous and forgiven

- ♥ Cared for

- ♥ Valuable and important.

We tell God who He is, and He in turn confirms who we are!

We must choose to bless the Lord at all times. Prayer

is not based on how we feel any particular day. Even in times of low faith or personal turmoil, our worship should be directed toward Him. Mark 11:24 states, "Whatever things you ask when you pray, believe that you receive them, and you will have them."

KINDS OF PRAYER

Beyond praise and worship, Scripture gives direction as we begin our time of prayer in the living room of our hearts. James 5:13-18 teaches us many types of prayers.

The Prayer of Faith

Faith is hoping, trusting and believing that the unseen will be seen. Scripture reveals, "And the prayer of faith will save the sick, and the Lord will raise him up. And if he has committed sins, he will be forgiven" (James 5:15). To have faith is to believe that the promises in God's Word are for you.

Our first prayer of faith was when we received God's salvation. Ephesians 2:8 states, "For by grace you have been saved through faith, and that not of yourselves; it is the gift of God." We repent of our sins and ask God to forgive us of our sins. But that shouldn't be our only prayer of faith in life. We can ask freely of anything from the Father, and He will answer our prayer of faith.

The Father assures us that it doesn't take much faith to see our prayers answered. In Matthew 17:20, Jesus said we need faith only as large as a grain of mustard seed.

That is the smallest of all seeds in Israel! It is minuscule, yet from the tiny seed grows a huge tree!

John 16:23 states, "Whatever you ask the Father in My name He will give you." Have faith—ask, trust and believe—and then thank God in advance that the answer is on the way!

Not long ago Lisa King, a young mother, asked for prayer for her newborn baby, whose heart was functioning at less than 10 percent. Worry gripped this new mother's heart, because the doctors expected death. The church as a corporate body, along with individual intercessors, began praying for little Morgan King.

A few weeks later, we hosted special speaker Ellen Parsley, Rod Parsley's mother, to come to minister to our congregation. During this anointed and supernatural night, the King family brought baby Morgan to Ellen Parsley for prayer. The whole family was under the power of God, and from that moment, the baby began to heal! One year later, at our annual women's conference "Taste the Glory," Lisa King and her 16-month-old healthy daughter, Morgan, were on stage giving God glory! Morgan's heart now functions at 80 percent, and even the doctors believe that God performed a miracle for her!

Prayer for the Afflicted

James 5:13 states, "Is any among you afflicted? let him pray. Is any merry? let him sing psalms" (KJV). This word *afflicted*, or *suffering*, means "to suffer badly or to be in an oppressive situation." We know that everyone has trials and difficulties. We cannot avoid times of pain, hurt, trouble and suffering. But turning them over to God in prayer should be our instinctive reaction.

Without thinking about it, when any little interruption or upheaval occurs I often say, "O Lord, help us!" I didn't realize how often I say this until recently when my 2-year-old grandson was staying with us. The last hour before he went home, every other phrase coming out of his sweet little mouth was "O Lord, help us!" It was humorous, but also struck home with me that this should be our attitude toward difficulty—instantly calling upon God in our need.

When we pray for ourselves and others who are suffering miserably, there are two prayers we should pray. First, ask for God to remove the affliction. Simply pray, "God, take it away. Let me get out of this dark valley." God hears your prayer, and many times He may say, "Yes, I will remove it. I will take it away. Through it, I will be honored and glorified."

Even when God says, "No, I will not remove this affliction," He promises that His grace is sufficient for you in this pain. Our second prayer should be to ask for God's grace to endure or walk through a situation. God reassures us that His grace will get us through hard times and that He will never leave or forsake us.

In Acts 16:23-26, we read where Paul and Silas were afflicted—suffering and in great trouble. These two missionaries were beaten with rods, shackled, bruised, bleeding, hurting, hungry, tired and thrown in prison. In the dark coldness of their prison cell, they did not know whether they would be dead or alive by morning, but they prayed and praised and worshiped God anyway! Along with their praise, I am sure their prayer was, "God, deliver us." And

God did! He sent an earthquake so all the chains fell off and the prison doors were opened!

Paul also experienced a "No" answer from God. We read in Scripture that Paul had a "thorn in [his] flesh" (2 Corithians 12:7). He was suffering severely. Some scholars believe Paul had an eye disease or physical malady. Others believe his problem may have actually been a group of people who were opposing and harassing him.

Whatever the cause of that "thorn," Paul prayed three times for God to remove it. But God said "No." Instead, God reassured Paul that His grace is always sufficient, "For My strength is made perfect in weakness" (v. 9).

Pray in times of trouble. Ask for deliverance. Ask for more grace to help you through every affliction. Whatever the outcome, you cannot lose!

Prayer of Intercession

Intercessory prayer is asking God to meet someone else's needs. Even now, the Lord Jesus Christ is at the right hand of the Father interceding for us, His followers. That means that 24 hours a day for seven days each week, Jesus is calling our name out to the Father!

We are commanded to pray earnestly and in faith, believing as we pray. When we intercede for others, we must focus on their needs.

In the Old Testament we read the story of Job, who was greatly afflicted. He lost his home, lands, flocks, herds, wealth, all 10 of his children, his health, and his life as he once knew it. The turning point came in Job 42:10 when God restored all of Job's losses. What preceded this turn-around? Job prayed for his friends! Immediately God gave him twice as much as he had had before!

Our church has a 24-hour prayer ministry. It is set up so that for a different assigned hour each week, members pray in their "living rooms of prayer." Needs are listed on prayer sheets and others are placed in a huge bowl on an altar table in our church. In addition, several intercessory groups meet at the church to pray. Individual intercessors pray for specific needs and specific ministries, countries and missionaries. They pray over requests from church members, as well as for the hundreds of prayer requests that come in from TV viewers each week.

Knowing someone is praying for us brings us such comfort and encouragement.

My husband and I both have intercessors who pray daily for us. James 5:16 states that "the effective, fervent [supplications] prayer of a righteous man avails much." Knowing someone is praying for us brings us such comfort and encouragement.

My dear mother is a great woman of faith—an example and an encouragement to me. She is a dynamic intercessor. Many nights God has awakened her to pray for others. Rarely does she know the seriousness or even any details of a situation, but she has learned to pray fervently until God releases her to stop.

During one of these wake-up calls from God, Mother

felt she should pray for a young dark-haired man in a pale blue shirt who was in great danger. She never saw his face—only the back of his head. She saw him in a hospital bed. As Mother prayed earnestly for his life, she didn't get a release to stop. Mother also saw a woman who wore beautiful rings and a bracelet standing beside the young man. Mother could only see her hand on the bed.

During this time of prayer on a Monday morning, my sister's son was driving from Tennessee to the University of Alabama. Just north of Birmingham, he went to sleep at the wheel and wrecked his car. When Mother arrived at the intensive care unit, she was amazed to find that my nephew had been wearing a pale blue shirt, and my sister's hand resting upon him was covered with rings and bracelets. Only then did Mother realize the urgency of her intercession. Praise the Lord, my nephew is fine, and thank God that Mother responded to the Lord's calling to pray!

Another time my mother was taking her daily walk in her neighborhood when she felt an intense burden to pray for my brother Dennis. Later that evening, she called my brother who, at that time, was delivering packages for UPS. She said, "What were you doing midway through the afternoon? I have been praying for you and I don't know why."

Dennis proceeded to tell her how, at that moment, he walked through the door of a business to find there was a robbery in progress! My brother ended up in a fight with the thief and had to appear in court as a witness. How we all thank God for a praying mother.

Prayer for the Sick

God cares about those who are sick and in need. "And the prayer of faith will save the sick, and the Lord will raise him up. And if he has committed sins, he will be forgiven" (James 5:15).

God promised that He would raise up the sick, if we pray the prayer of faith. We should not worry about how, when and where the person will be healed. God does the healing. Hebrews 13:8 says that Jesus "is the same yesterday, today, and forever." When He was on earth, He touched and healed many. And today, He still does. Jesus has not changed!

A friend of mine who is suffering from cancer has been the focus of my prayer for several months. My prayer team has prayed for her. Our intercessors at church have prayed for her. Other women who suffered the same affliction have prayed for her.

The Bible teacher from our school went with me to her home last February and shared the gospel with her. My dear friend asked Jesus to forgive her sins and be the Lord and authority of her life. But still she suffered from her affliction.

This precious teacher friend had breast cancer and lymphoma. The doctors gave her a 30 percent chance of survival. She went through chemotherapy. She was bald, weak and very sick. She had to return to teaching, because she is the only provider for her family. Even without strength, in September she endured 25 days of radiation. When I saw how badly burned her body was, I cried. It was painful for her to wear clothing for several days because of the intense burns.

I visited her every week, so I became close to the situation. I knew she was facing a critical visit with some specialists. God had already impressed on me to pray over her, to lay hands on her and to anoint her with oil. I was willing to do this. But the Scripture says to let the person who is sick ask to be prayed over and anointed with oil (James 5:14). So I waited. After a death in her family, she called me and said, "Paulette, will you come and lay hands on me and anoint me with oil and pray?" Of course, I said yes!

Following her appointment on Thursday, I anxiously waited for her phone call. I knew if she received a bad report, an ambulance would take her straight to Nashville for a stem-cell, bone marrow transplant. The survival rate for the procedure is only about 5 percent. But as I picked up the phone, I heard her shouting: the doctors had pronounced her in remission! She did not even have to return for a check-up for six months. She cried, laughed, danced and shouted, "Thank You, Lord!" She knew God had raised her up.

Alfred Lord Tennyson, a poet laureate of England (1850-1892), said, "More things have been wrought through prayer than the world has ever dreamed of."

When you pray, expect an answer. When you ask, expect God to heal. Believe what God said He would do. Find and claim the promises in the Bible for yourself. Take your promises from God daily, just like you take your vitamins. His promises are your prescription for spiritual health and maturity.

It is important to understand some things about what the Scriptures do NOT say about healing. Scripture does not teach that God will heal *all* people who are sick. I don't

understand why everyone is not healed physically, but
God does. Of course, heaven is the ultimate healing.
Sickness and death are our transportation to heaven.

Second, Scripture does not condemn medicine or the
medical profession. God uses the medical profession
just as much as He uses His divine, supernatural,
instant healing.

How do we know that from Scripture? One evidence is
the active work of Luke, the physician, in the ministry of
Paul. Second Timothy 4:11 reminds us that Luke, the
beloved physician, was with Paul. They worked together as
a team. In Acts 28, Luke was by his side when Paul laid
hands on and prayed for Publius' father. He was healed and
restored to his normal life. Verses 9 and 10 tell us that other
people on the island were being healed. The word *healing*
in the Greek actually refers to "therapy." This means that
Luke was using his medical ability to heal people.

Third, this passage does not require all people to ask
for healing. This passage says, "Let the sick ask." This
does not limit the power of God in healing.

Prayer of Confession

James 5:16 gives us an important reminder: "Confess
your faults one to another, and pray one for another, that ye
may be healed. The effectual fervent prayer of a righteous
man availeth much" (KJV). This passage introduces the
subject of sin in our prayers. Sin separates. We cannot have
a right relationship with God until our sins are forgiven.

First John 1:9 reminds us, "If we confess our sins [to
God], He is faithful and just to forgive us our sins and to

cleanse us from all unrighteousness." If we confess to God that we have committed wrongs, then God will forgive us and remove our sin as far away as the east is from the west and will NEVER remember our wrongs again!

In the quietness of our prayer time, God may reveal to us our faults against others. He will prompt us to set things right and ask others for forgiveness. Be quick to forgive and ask for forgiveness! A good rule of thumb is this: If the sin is committed publicly, a public confession is in order. But if a sin is committed in private, confession should be made privately.

Seek the Quiet Place

As you seek to establish your "living room of prayer," remember that prayer must be persistent. Prayer is a weapon against the Evil One, so pray at home. Pray without stopping. Pray at work, pray at church, and pray on vacation. Pray privately and publicly. As you pray, you will bring the resources of heaven into every situation and every problem of your life. God will answer your prayer. What He promised, He will do!

Review Questions

1. When is your best time to pray?

2. Where did Jesus pray in Mark 1:35?

3. How was our Lord Jesus Christ a role model for our prayer life? Review each of these prayers of Jesus and uncover what He was preparing for or about to do:

   Luke 6:12, 13

   Luke 9:16

   John 11: 41-43

   Luke 22: 40-45

   Luke 23:34, 46; Mark 15:34

   John 17

4. Study the model prayer in Matthew 6:9-13. What part of this prayer is most meaningful to you?

5. How do praise and worship differ?

6. Praise is bragging on what God has done. Write down something God has done for you this past month.

7. Worship is celebrating the character of God. Try this in your next time of worship in prayer: Take the letters of the alphabet, and use each letter as the first in a word of praise for what God has done. For example, "I praise God for answered prayer, for being my bread daily, for being the Creator of all." Next, take the alphabet and use each letter to begin a word about who God is. Example: "I worship God as ageless, anointed, my Abba Father; for being the Balm of Gilead, the Bridegroom, blessed; my Cornerstone, the living Christ," and so forth.

8. Give an example either from your life or from the discussion in this chapter for each type of prayer:

   ᛨ Prayer of Faith (John 16:23; Ephesians 2:8)

   ᛨ Prayer for the Afflicted (James 5:13)

   ᛨ Prayer of Intercession (James 5:16)

   ᛨ Prayer for the Sick (Jeremiah 33:3; James 5:15)

   ᛨ Prayer of Confession (James 5:16; 1 John 1:9)

"Ships that pass in the night,
and speak to each other in passing,
Only a signal shown,
and a distant voice in the darkness;
So on the ocean of life,
we pass and speak one to another,
Only a look and a voice,
then darkness again and a silence."
—Henry Wadsworth Longfellow

"To dare to live alone is the rarest courage;
since there are many who had rather meet their
bitterest enemy in the field,
than their own hearts in their closet."
—Charles Caleb Colton

3

The Back Porch of Loneliness

My first experience of separation was when I was 17. As the oldest of six children, I never had a moment of loneliness growing up in our bustling and noisy home! Since I had never really been away from home, except to visit extended family, I was apprehensive when the time came for me to go away to college.

One Sunday, my parents unloaded me and most of my treasures into my 11-by-13-foot dormitory room at Samford University, said tearful farewells, and quietly drove off campus in the direction of home. Even though home was only two hours down the road, it seemed to be a world away!

There I was—alone in a strange town, in a new environment, without a car or a friend. My roommate, who was a senior, would not arrive for five days. Nausea churned in my stomach and I was instantly homesick. I thought, *Maybe I've made a mistake and can't make it on my own.* I'll never forget those first few days of being by myself, far away from the support of my family.

A second bout of loneliness came before and after the

birth of my second daughter, Heather. At the time, we lived in New Orleans, Louisiana, which was the proverbial 500 miles away from my hometown. We had little money. My husband worked two jobs while earning his doctorate at New Orleans Baptist Theological Seminary, and his life was filled with study and hard work.

The feeling of hopelessness and loneliness is no respecter of persons.

I needed help in many areas, but most of all, I missed my parents and far-away friends. I needed someone to say I was a good mother and was doing things right. I needed encouragement as a homemaker, a wife and a pastor's wife. In those days, a pastor's wife was not supposed to have close friends in the church or share personal needs or inadequacies. The fear was that whatever prayer requests were shared would become the gossip mill's story of the week! My bout with loneliness is one that many pastors' wives share.

Forgotten by the World

Do you have a back porch on your home? Many homes have a back deck or porch that becomes a catch-all for seasonal paraphernalia like swim gear, garden hoses, snow skis and poles, and other items that are no longer needed. Perhaps a wilted potted plant or two attempt to bring some cheer to the space, but it is easy for the back porch to reflect neglect, with an air of "better days have gone by."

This type of back porch is not one we want to have spiritually. Sitting there on the back porch of our loneliness, we look around at the broken dreams, abandoned in a corner. The feeling of hopelessness and loneliness is no respecter of persons. It attacks the young and the old, the strong and the weak, the busy and the indolent, the married and the divorced, the rich and the poor, the single parent and the widower. This feeling makes us think no one cares or loves us.

We can be thankful that most people only struggle with temporary bouts of loneliness. Like me, you may have suffered as a young wife and mother with babies, confined in a metropolitan area far away from support. Maybe you underwent a big job change and moved cross-country.

Perhaps you are a single adult who prays for a friend to enter your life . . . someone to just call and talk to or "hang out" with for an hour. Maybe you are an "empty nester" whose home is quiet for the first time in 20 years. The house is so clean that you wish the football team or the high school band would show up, eat pizza and just trash the place! Even more painful, perhaps, is the deep loss of losing your spouse, your only companion.

Luke 4:18 states that Jesus came to set free those who are downtrodden. Has sickness, a wheelchair or a doctor's bad report forced you into isolation? Are you the only Christian in your family and feel frustrated about sharing your faith? Or perhaps since you took a stand and spoke out at work, you don't fit in with the crowd anymore and workdays are endless. No matter the source of your loneliness, you know that it is impossible to hide from the pain.

Ways We Cope With Loneliness

Feelings of loneliness draw us to others. Desperately wanting to be a part of a group—to fit in and not stand out as an obvious outsider or outcast—we are compelled to find friends.

Some people try alcohol and drugs to dull the pain, or at least to forget it for a while. Others flock to bars. How many bars and nightclubs are in your town? The television comedy *Cheers* extolled a bar as the place "where everybody knows your name." Notice that the parking lots at these clubs are always full.

Television, soap operas, novels and movies attract the lonely to a life of escapism. These beckon you to live vicariously in the fantasy of those you watch or read about.

Mood swings and depression are by-products of loneliness and, when left unchecked, they can lead to suicidal tendencies. Realize that Jesus came to set free those who are downtrodden.

The Lonely Walk of Jesus

Scripture teaches us that Jesus suffered in all ways—just as we suffer. He was God who became a man, so He could pay for our sins. Imagine how lonely earth was compared to the wonders of heaven, which was filled with the glory of God the Father and the entire heavenly host. The man who wrote "One Solitary Life" was right. Jesus died alone. None of those who had received His ministry or miracles were near Him at the cross.

Jesus was without companions or friends. He even shouted from the cross, "My God, My God, why have

You forsaken Me?" (Matthew 27:46; Mark 15:34). As the beloved hymn says:

Jesus paid it all,
All to Him I owe;
Sin had left a crimson stain;
He washed it white as snow.

He knew all our pain. That is why His Word promises us in Hebrews 13:5, "I will never leave you nor forsake you."

Sometimes God designs the alone times to instruct us and to bless us.

"Alone" Is Not "Lonely"

It is important for us to realize that God plans alone times to be times of instruction, purpose and focus. God often isolates us to be alone with Him. Our God is a jealous God who wants us to seek Him with our whole heart. Don't confuse being alone with being lonely. God instructs us to "be still, and know that I am God" (Psalm 46:10). Determine not to despise or be uncomfortable in these times, because they are for our good.

Many Bible characters experienced these times of isolation. In Genesis 28, Jacob was sleeping alone on a rock pillow when God gave him a vision of a ladder leading to heaven, with angels going up and down. In 32:24, Jacob was left alone to wrestle with a man until the breaking of the day. Jacob was touched in the thigh so that he limped the rest of his life, but this man/angel blessed Jacob with a new name, Israel, before he left. Sometimes God designs the alone times to instruct us and to bless us.

In Exodus 3:1-6, Moses was alone with his sheep on the back side of the desert at Mount Horeb when God showed him a burning bush and gave him a mission to return to Egypt and lead the Israelites to freedom. It was God's purpose for Moses to be alone to hear His voice and obey His assignment.

The great prophet Isaiah was alone in his grief over the death of King Uzziah. It was in this "alone" season that Isaiah rushed to the Holy of Holies in great despair, desperate for answers from God. Entering the Holy of Holies could have meant death for Isaiah, yet God was merciful, revealed His glory and His holiness, and gave Isaiah a new vision and commission in life (Isaiah 6:1-9).

As already mentioned, Jesus experienced many times of isolation. He went alone into the wilderness and was tempted by the Enemy. But Jesus was always the victor. Scripture tells us that Jesus would often get up from sleep a "a long while before daylight" to be alone with the Father and pray (Mark 1:35).

Peter was alone on the rooftop when he saw the heavenly vision about unclean animals. He needed to be alone in order to hear God's voice, for his new mission was to take the gospel to Cornelius and the Gentiles (see Acts 10:9-20). Alone times are for our well-being, our benefit, our yielding and our instruction to God's assignment.

After a rebellious and disobedient time, the prophet Jonah found himself for three days and three nights in the belly of a great fish (see Jonah 1:1-17). Jonah had three days of isolation to reflect on his sin. Can you imagine how he must have feared for his life with every passing minute? He must have cowered fearfully in that dark abyss. The roar of the seas and the swells of the waves must have dizzied him in every movement. In chapter 2, he calls the place the "belly of Sheol" (v. 2), literally a hell of death and darkness.

The residue of the sea wrapped around Jonah's filthy body as the seaweed tangled his hair. The stench of undigested sea matter must have been nauseating. If ever a man believed his life was ending, it was surely Jonah as he cried for mercy and promised to obey God's assignment. When he hit the sand of the seashore, how thankful he must have been!

Jonah's experience gave him back his life, yet it changed his life forever, and the life of a whole nation. He purposed in his heart to serve God and live for God. God preserved him—freed, delivered and commissioned Jonah once again in his time of isolation. God wanted Jonah to learn that satisfaction and purpose for this life can only be found in Him.

When times of isolation come, we are removed from all hindrances. No friends or colleagues call to relieve our stress. No welcome interference comes as a diversion from God's truth. That includes food, the mall, books, television, music or hobbies. God requires our undivided attention.

Mother Teresa said, "Loneliness and the feeling of being unwanted is the most terrible poverty." Not long ago, I knew a teacher who was in a difficult marriage, then separated and ultimately divorced. Her first reaction to loneliness was to buy a dog. This helped, but of course it wasn't enough. So my friend began going once a month to a spa for a massage or a facial because she simply needed a human touch. In addition, she finally learned that when she felt lonely, she could find great comfort in God.

You can find direction, strength and guidance in the Bible, which is food for the soul, your bread of life, and water from the rock.

John 15 reminds us to abide in Christ and He will abide in us (see vv. 15-21). We can know God intimately as a friend that "sticks closer than a brother" (Proverbs 18:24). We can know Jesus in the power of His resurrection.

What to Do in Lonely Times

It is possible to make the back porch a place of refuge. I love to seek God on my back porch early in the morning. When I see the sun come up, I am energized. When I hear the birds harmonizing, I cannot help but let my spirit soar. When I smell the honeysuckles and feel the gentle wind or noisy rain, I remind myself of God's mercy that is new each morning. If I get up later when the sun is already scorching, I truly miss that restful morning solitude with God.

I go to the back porch to hear from God's Word. In studying the Bible, I find strength for whatever the day holds. I find encouragement. Psalm 119:50 states, "This is my comfort in my affliction, for Your word has given me life." You can find direction, strength and guidance in the Bible, which is food for the soul, your bread of life, and water from the rock. Without its spiritual sustenance, we are unhealthy in our spirit.

We don't have to be lonely! The God of the universe, through the salvation of His Son, Jesus, and the indwelling of His Holy Spirit, wants to keep a divine appointment with us any day and every day—any time or all the time. God tells us that we can "come boldly to the throne of grace, that we may obtain mercy and find grace to help in time of need" (Hebrews 4:16). We have an audience with God whenever we desire it.

In the Old Testament, we have the account of young David, a shepherd boy, on a hillside with a few sheep. During those lonely times on the "back porch" of his hillside, David became a "man after God's own heart" because he prayed, sang, worshiped, danced and communicated with God in every way he knew.

Back Porch of Blessing

On my back porch, I pray. When the problems of life seem to suffocate me, I pray and cry out to God, and He always listens. When despair or problems are paramount, God replaces them with hope and joy. When I pray about fears, God restores my peace. Oftentimes I cry out about unfair circumstances and difficult situations. The circumstances don't always change, but through prayer, I am able to change.

I can settle most of the issues of my life on my back

porch. I go there because I need to be alone. I don't see a messy house when I am on the porch. I don't take a telephone to my porch! I certainly don't take my calendar to check the agenda for the day. I go to the back porch to be alone. In the privacy of my back porch, I pour out my heart to God, I lay down my difficulties, and there I learn obedience and submission.

In the spring several years ago, I was on my back porch praying about some major decisions and hurts in my life. In many ways, this was a crucial season. It was not the first time I had earnestly prayed to God concerning all these major ordeals; however, on this day, something different happened. A new and deeper presence of the Holy Spirit was with me. The Scripture teaches that the Spirit prays for us in "groanings which cannot be uttered" (Romans 8:26). I was too burdened even to voice my prayers to God, but the Holy Spirit began to release in me a new prayer language. As I prayed in these new expressions, syllables, words, sentences and paragraphs, I felt a release from my care. Such great joy enveloped me that I began to laugh, and I laughed and laughed. It was a good thing that I was alone on my porch, because no one would have understood what happened that morning! His ways are not our ways, and He does all things well.

Am I better because of that experience? Yes, and I repeat, *yes*! In John 14:18, Jesus promised, "I will not leave you comfortless [lonely, orphaned]: I will come to you" (KJV). In my hour of need and feeling alone in a sea of trouble, God met me on my back porch and released new life into me.

The next time you sense loneliness, seek contentment with God, who loves you. He will meet you on the back porch and fill your life with companionship and love.

Review Questions

1. List the times of greatest loneliness in your own life. Relate how God brought you through each of those experiences.

2. What are the basic emotions or feelings that occurred during your time of loneliness?

3. What do you think is the loneliest experience a Christian can have?

4. As discussed in this chapter, what are the differences between aloneness and loneliness?

5. What can you let God accomplish in your times of aloneness?

6. How did the following individuals benefit from times of aloneness with God?

   Abraham

   Jacob

   Moses

   Elijah

Isaiah

David

Jonah

Peter

Jesus

7. Review the following Scripture references, and commit one to memory as a source of comfort when you find yourself on the back porch of loneliness:

Matthew 6:31

Proverbs 18:10

Psalm 25:16, 17

Hosea 2:14, 15

Psalm 142:3, 4

Hebrews 13:5

John 14:18

Psalm 46:1

Romans 8:35-39

"His mouth is most sweet, yes, he is altogether lovely.
This is my beloved, and this is my friend"
(Song of Solomon 5:16).

How do I love thee? Let me count the ways.
I love thee to the depth and breadth and height
My soul can reach, when feeling out of sight
For the ends of Being and ideal Grace.
I love thee to the level of every day's
Most quiet need, by sun and candlelight.
I love thee freely, as men strive for Right
I love thee purely, as they turn from Praise.
I love thee with the passion put to use
In my old griefs, and with my childhood's faith.
I love thee with a love I seemed to lose
With my lost saints. I love thee with the breath,
Smiles, tears, of all my life. And, if God choose,
I shall but love thee better after death.
—Elizabeth Barrett Browning
43 *Songs of the Portuguese*

4

The Bedroom of Intimacy

heart that is satisfied is intimate first with God. We read in Scripture, "God is love" (1 John 4:8). God defines the very essence of love. He reveals the very nature of love when He loved us unconditionally. Without knowing God, we will never truly experience the love God created us to know. Loving God is the most passionate, intimate love humankind is capable of knowing. God loves you as an individual. He loved you before the foundation of the world, and His love is forever. There is no substitute for this love.

Loving and knowing God is foundational in your life. Our love for God must be passionate, intense and without demands or conditions, because "perfect love casts out fear" (v. 18). Perfect love is lavished on another without hoping for anything in return. We were created with a God-shaped void in our lives to love and be intimate with the God of the universe. James 4:8 declares, "Draw near to God and He will draw near to you." Psalm 25:14 states, "The secret of the Lord is with those who fear

Him." This word *secret* means "counsel or intimacy." When we are intimate, we share secrets.

Intimacy could be defined as "belonging, warm, private, friendship, caring, trust, giving, informal nature, thoughtfulness—to sit down together, counsel, instruct, establish, settle and share inward secrets." When we desire intimacy with God, we expect Him to satisfy and fulfill our needs. We then have an indescribable peace and joy no human being can provide. If you are single or widowed, you can still have the greatest intimacy. Proverbs 3:32 declares, "He is intimate with the upright" (*NASB*).

When we desire intimacy with God, we expect Him to satisfy and fulfill our needs.

Hollywood portrays intimacy as a one-night stand. "Casual sex" on the movie screen has changed the moral culture of America. A popular song teaches us that if you can't be with the one you love, love the one you're with! This is not intimacy; it is devastation and emotional destruction.

Our human relationships reflect our relationship with God. Our human relationships will be as healthy, rewarding and, yes, intimate. There is a place in your heart for intimacy with God, with others and with your mate. Before we can enhance intimacy in the bedroom, we must know what men and women desire in this most private of rooms.

Walter Harley is a noted author and marriage counselor.

He helps thousands through his support information found at *www.marriagebuilders.com*. He proposes that a husband's basic needs in marriage include admiration from his wife, sexual gratification, recreational companionship, an attractive spouse, and vocational and domestic support of his needs and dreams. A wife's basic needs in marriage include affection and attention, honest and open conversation, financial support, a spiritual leader, and family commitment.

Sexual incompatibility is still the number one reason for divorce. The bedroom is the place to strengthen the bonds of marriage and make the needs of both mates a top priority. Unfortunately, Christians shy away from this subject. But God has a lot to say about it.

Keys to Intimacy

Let's focus on larger issues of intimacy and romance in the bedroom of your heart and home. An acrostic for the word *intimate* helps us set the stage for romance.

Inviting

Nurturing

Transparency

Intensity

Model

Appreciation

Trust

Expectations

Inviting

Our mothers drilled into us the importance of a neat, tidy bedroom. Having a warm, inviting and appealing bedroom does a lot for our own spirits, but I believe it is also important in developing intimacy with our spouses. Is your bedroom attractive and appealing to both of you? Is the bed made, or do you have clothes lying around with discarded magazines, newspapers, accumulated mail or bills, medicines or piles of papers from work? Is it the last room you clean up? If you can afford to decorate only one room in your home, let it be the bedroom!

In my own home, I first decorated the whole house with shades of pink, my favorite color! My dear husband bravely went along with my decisions and never complained. However, a few years ago, I redecorated our bedroom to reflect a more Mediterranean style, with muted greens and golds. Every inch of the room seems to be calling, "Come relax—unwind!" My husband was thrilled with the new masculine touches!

Music and candles are a calming touch in a bedroom. I like to place a tray on the bed with flowers or pictures. The bedroom should be an inviting and welcoming retreat to focus on each other and shut everything else out.

Scripture has some very careful advice for those who are married:

> Let the husband render to his wife the affection due her, and likewise also the wife to her husband. The wife does not have authority over her own body, but the husband does. And likewise the husband does not have authority over his own body, but the wife does. Do not deprive

one another except with consent for a time, that you may give yourselves to fasting and prayer; and come together again so that Satan does not tempt you because of your lack of self-control (1 Corinthians 7:3-5).

Nurturing

What you share with your mate in intimacy should be mutually satisfying. It can be adventurous, but you should experiment only when you both agree. Wear bedroom attire that is appealing . . . throw away those worn-out faded flannels! Clothing communicates your mood. Your attitude, conversation and behavior will help shape an inviting evening.

Proverbs 31:12 states, "She does him good and not evil all the days of her life." How do we nurture our husbands? We nurture him the same way we nurture our children. Indeed, marital intimacy is the foundation for the family. We nurture with soothing words that communicate tenderness, empathy, encouragement, comfort, love, calmness and peace. We can go a long time on a positive, uplifting word of praise. A kind word can turn your day around! Remember though that words are easily spoken, but rarely forgotten. Negative words can unfortunately be remembered for a lifetime.

Another way to nurture is through our actions. Over time and through experience, you learn what actions best speak to your husband's needs. Maybe holding his hand sustains him. At times, a back massage or foot rub can take away the day's tension. His favorite comfort foods can help him relax. Ask him this question, "What can I do to make you feel really loved?" You might be surprised at his answer.

My husband brings coffee to me in bed every morning. I enjoy that first cup in bed so I can wake up slowly. That simple act lets me know my needs are important to him. Breakfast in bed pampers me.

Create a comfortable surrounding. Home should be a haven and a fortress from the rest of the world.

A third way to nurture is through creating a comfortable surrounding. Peace and quiet are important at home. Home should be a haven and a fortress from the rest of the world. Don't bombard your spouse with all the day's woes as soon as he walks in the door; give your husband 30 minutes to unwind and change clothes after work.

A comfortable, relaxed atmosphere at home brings with it security, calm, peace and rest, and promotes harmony. Fatigue, tension and stress make us say and do things we may regret. Times of refreshing are needed for everyone in the family.

Transparency

Psalm 91 states that truth shall be a shield (see v. 4). Open and honest communication refuses to allow walls of secrets to be erected in your marriage. Be positive and a good listener. The Bible says, "[Speak] the truth in love" (Ephesians 4:15) and "Do not let the sun go down on your wrath" (v. 26). Avoid finishing his sentences, interrupting him or correcting him. Honor his thoughts and opinions.

Time with each other is essential if open dialogue is to take place. With today's hectic pace, often all we speak are surface questions and answers. Getting to know your mate deeply takes a lifetime. Praying with each other and for each other produces such oneness of spirit that there is no room for guile or pretense left in your relationship. Let your husband hear you bring his name and needs to God in prayer.

Intensity

In a recently published book I coauthored with my husband, Ron, *Invitation to Intimacy*, we walked through the Book of Song of Solomon and studied the descriptions of intimate love and commitment pictured there, relating them to the intimacy we can know with God. In Song of Solomon 4 and 5, the actual act of intimacy is described. In our study, we stated the following:

The consummation is an intimate relationship in its highest form. In all of literature—sacred and secular—this is the most beautiful of all love scenes. It is handled delicately and discreetly, and yet it is forthright.

That beautiful relationship was possible because of a beautiful courtship. The high intensity of their passion was possible because their love had been deepened by courtship. No long session of "making out" had taken the fulfilling excitement from their honeymoon night. Overfamiliarity had not dulled the intensity of their desire. They did not "awaken love till it was time" (see 2:7; 3:5; 8:4).

The process described in Song of Solomon involves the woman desiring her husband, the couple satisfied in the act of marriage, and then the voice of God putting His stamp of approval on their union. "Eat, O friends! Drink, yes, and drink deeply, O beloved ones!" (5:1). God says enjoy and have fun in marital love.

Model

I am blessed to have a husband who is a true romantic. While we were dating, Ron worked as a delivery boy for the best florist in town. I received flowers every week and for every occasion! In addition, he is an avid gift-giver. Twice, he has bought me music boxes with special songs.

One very special surprise followed a very difficult health crisis for me. Ron whisked me away to California for a week! This was such a treat, because we had never been there and because he planned it all by himself. Usually, I plan the details of our trips, but this time he went selflessly outside his comfort zone and planned everything—even purchasing tickets to see the *Phantom of the Opera*. Although I wasn't very strong physically, I had an unforgettable time.

If your husband isn't particularly romantic, you can be the one to model intimacy to him. If he doesn't send you flowers, you can send him flowers! Several years ago on Valentine's Day, I had a balloon bouquet and a singing telegram delivered to Ron at the church. A clown sang,

"You Are My Sunshine" to him with most of the staff looking on! He loved it.

If you are traveling, put a card under his pillow for him to find while you are away. If he travels, put little surprises in his suitcase. This communicates, "I am thinking of you; I miss you, and you are important to me."

The Golden Rule teaches us, "Do unto others as you would have them do unto you" (see Matthew 7:12). I was blessed to be able to surprise my husband with a trip to the British Open Golf Tournament. My girlfriend and I planned for a whole year to honor our husbands with this trip. My husband was as giddy as a child when he found out! We treasured every moment of the trip. Even though it was a year ago, he never tires of talking about it. He still says it was a highlight of his life.

There is nothing wrong with educating each other about your likes and dislikes—you each need reminding now and then. Remember to thank your husband every time he does something special. Keep dating each other. A date night is necessary, no matter how long you have been married. Make time for romance and intimacy. When we were younger, we decided never to talk about major issues or bills after 9 p.m. Fatigue and stress would cause an argument that late. Spend time with your husband. When you have children, spending intimate time

> *A date night is necessary, no matter how long you have been married. Make time for romance and intimacy.*

takes creativity, but teaching your kids that a locked door means "leave us alone" will help.

Appreciation

Just as a woman blossoms with affection, romance and attention—a man finds strength when he is appreciated, admired and respected. A man loves to know that his own wife thinks that he is a success, that he has integrity, that he is a good provider, a good husband and a good father. Words of admiration should fill your mouth rather than words of criticism.

We all thrive on praise and sincere compliments. Even the Scripture says that God inhabits the praises of His people (see Psalm 22:3). My children love for me to brag on them. My grandchildren love to hear me praise them. From the time they could sit alone, we would clap and say "Yeah" at every new antic they learned. Everyone loves to hear a compliment of praise from a superior at work or from our friends. And your mate is no different. He needs to know he is doing a good job, making good decisions and achieving worthwhile goals.

I realize that respect and appreciation must be earned. When it is difficult to give praise, then remember the past and give praise for your husband's strength in better times. Even in difficult times, your husband needs unconditional love, unwavering faith, support and your belief that he is great.

Proverbs 31:26 tells us, "She opens her mouth with wisdom, and on her tongue is the law of kindness." Appreciation is the expression of a grateful heart. Simple kindness and good manners go a long way to encourage your mate. Remember to brag or praise your mate publicly—in front of your children, to his parents and to yours. *Agape* love is doing what is best, not what is deserved.

If you don't appreciate your mate, someone else will. The more you respect and admire him, the greater person he will become.

Trust

Proverbs 31:11 states, "The heart of her husband safely trusts in her." Trust is an element in your intimacy and friendship that assures you that your inner secrets are secure. As your best friend, your spouse should protect your trust, confidence and faith. Your mate should be able to feel secure that you will not betray him in thought or action. As Proverbs 3:5, 6 says, "Trust in the Lord . . . and lean not on your own understanding. In all your ways acknowledge Him, and He shall direct your paths."

Our Lord never fails and always is working for our best. We should pattern our relationships after His faithfulness to us. Maybe our mate will never be perfect like Christ, but as we grow in our relationship, the trust level should be full. Trust your mate to do what is right, to say

If you don't appreciate your mate, someone else will. The more you respect and admire him, the greater person he will become.

what is right, to keep that which is holy, and to be faithful to your marriage.

Perhaps you have had past experiences that have caused you to lose trust in your mate. Without trust, a marriage cannot grow. Can you turn over the difficulties to God and learn to trust again? Yes, you can. When trust is broken, forgive, put away the hurt and start again. Every relationship must do that regularly in order to grow.

"Love . . . bears all things, believes all things, hopes all things, endures all things. Love never fails" (1 Corinthians 13:4, 7, 8).

Expectations

You cannot meet every need of your husband's life; nor can your husband meet every need of your life. You may each try tirelessly, but you will fail, because only God can supply every need. You may see your husband as your "knight in shining armor," but he cannot correct every wrong or make every situation perfect for you.

Sometimes when your mate gets so frustrated because he cannot do enough, say enough, or be enough, he may quit trying. His actions are like raindrops falling in a very deep barrel. He will get to the point that he cannot make you happy. He no longer knows what to do, so he is not going to try anymore. This responsibility is too much for any human being.

If your expectations are too high, focus on Philippians 4:19: "My God shall supply all your needs according to His riches in glory." Our God is the provider in our lives, and Jesus Christ is the lifter of our heads.

A Tower of Strength

Proverbs 18:10 says, "The name of the Lord is a strong tower; the righteous run to it and are safe." When you are in the tower of strength, you will find He lifts you above the cares of personal needs.

Not long ago, my husband and I ventured to the very apex of the Eiffel Tower in Paris. As the huge glass elevator climbed higher and higher, we soared above rooftops, church spires and skyscrapers. Large, flowing rivers appeared as tiny streams snaking through the grand old town. Trains and automobiles were crawling like tiny model cars. Yet, we were far above it all. Our vantage point was so high above the city that things below seemed small, removed and insignificant.

When we run to the strong tower of God, we are safe, things are in perspective, and the cares of this world seem insignificant.

When we run to the strong tower of God, we are safe, things are in perspective, and the cares of this world seem insignificant. There is a bigger perspective than our personal needs.

Your husband cannot be God for you. Be who you are and ask God to change what needs to be changed in you and in your husband. Free your husband to be all he can be in Christ. Psalm 62:5 states, "My soul, wait silently for God alone, for my expectation is from Him."

If we get our eyes off God and on our husbands, we force

our husbands to be accountable for our needs, moods and desires. If you exist in a codependent cycle, your relationship will not grow, but it will be stifled, choked, consumed and defeated. You do have God-given needs that only your husband can meet, but God alone can meet the vast majority of needs. We are all needy people, but most of all, we need God. What a joy to know He never tires of meeting our needs. Look to God for contentment, peace and joy. Ask God to free your mate from your petty needs. Ask God to make your husband the great man of God he can be. Ask God to free you to be a woman of faith in Christ.

Intimacy is not about locating the perfect mate—it is about becoming the right person. Commit yourself today to be the best you can be in your marriage. Perhaps you can take one or more of these steps today:

- ♥ Staying sexually pure if you are not currently married
- ♥ Making your marriage the number one priority of your life after Christ
- ♥ Committing to pray daily for your mate
- ♥ Deciding to never threaten with the word *divorce*
- ♥ Breaking off an affair immediately if you are in an adulterous relationship

Intimacy is attainable with God and your mate. Intimacy in body is the sexual physical union. Intimacy of soul includes mind, will and emotions. Intimacy of spirit is union in worship, prayer and servanthood—putting the needs of the other above our own.

The best example of *agape* love is what Christ did for

us on the cross of Calvary. He poured out His life out of love for us. He took every weakness and every sin in His body, because He loved us when we did not deserve or merit His love. Love that is deserved is conditional love. Our God loved us without conditions. Show love to your husband for who he is. He won't be your favorite actor on some movie screen, he cannot be someone else, and some things he cannot change, but love him for who he is. He will never be perfect, but he is God's perfect gift to you.

Review Questions

1. Love is hard work. A great marriage is not in locating the right mate but in becoming the right person! You must love yourself before you can love another. Privately write a philosophy or game plan for your life. Fill in the chart:

   Personality strengths

   Personality weaknesses

   Goals for your marriage growth

2. How does the dictionary define *intimacy*?

3. List by personal experiences, ways you can . . .
   Accept your husband

   Admire your husband

   Adapt to your husband

   Appreciate your husband

   Activate sex with your husband.

4. Listed below is an acrostic for *intimate*. Explain how you can incorporate these in your experiences with your mate.

Inviting (1 Corinthians 7:3-5)

Nurturing (Proverbs 31:12)

Transparency

Intensity (Song of Solomon 4:16; 5:1)

Model

Appreciation (Ephesians 5:33)

    Psalm 37:3

    Proverbs 3:5

    Micah 7:5

    Psalm 32:10

    Proverbs 31:11

Trust (Proverbs 31:11)

Expectations (Psalm 62:8)

"Behold, children are a heritage from the Lord,
The fruit of the womb is a reward.
Like arrows in the hand of a warrior,
So are the children of one's youth.
Happy is the man who has his quiver full of them"
(Psalm 127:3-5).

5

The Playroom of Parenting

In the middle of labor pains with our first child, my floodgate of tears revealed me to be a giddy, first-time mother who was suddenly struck with a fear of looming responsibility. Few joys compare to what I felt when I held my baby in my arms for the first time in the hospital. My mother wisely said, "You have just experienced your greatest joy and your deepest pain!"

Even now as my three children have children of their own, I am filled repeatedly with joy, awe, euphoria and supreme love—not only in the pride of watching my own children embrace the joys of parenthood, but also at the newfound blessings of being a grandparent! Proverbs 17:6 states: "Children's children are the crown of old men, and the glory of children is their father."

My three children would admit that they lived in a fish bowl of scrutiny in the public eye as pastor's kids. To be honest, I didn't always handle that very well myself! If I had it to do over, I would always operate in our standards and never worry about what other people thought or expected of us.

Whether you are a single person who assists in day care or nursery, a newlywed who is looking forward to the joys of parenthood, a mother with growing and active children or teens, or a grandparent who is warmed by the embrace of a chubby-faced grandchild, I want to walk you through the playroom of parenting in this chapter. I do not intend to be an expert and tell you how to raise children. Childbearing and parenting are wonderful and joyous experiences, but both can be complicated.

You are responsible before God for nurturing your children spiritually and teaching them about God.

My pastor husband, Ron, and I did many things right with our children, but we made mistakes as well. In looking back, I believe our problem was not with our children, but the problem was with me! I bought into the lie that my children should be perfect in the eyes of the church. That is too much pressure for any family, and it is wrong for a church to put its leaders' families on a pedestal.

Designing the Playroom

Parents are the general contractors of the home. You are building a physical family and a spiritual home. Your goal is to raise your children to be spiritually, mentally and emotionally strong adults. This role is specifically yours. You may allow yourself to "loan out" parts of child raising, such as education, sports, music lessons or ballet, but you are ultimately responsible for the education of your child. Don't trust any person with the sole responsibility for your child's welfare. You are responsible before God for nurturing your children spiritually and teaching them about God. The church will help you, but you must not pass the buck.

A good illustration of our responsibility to our children is given a thousand times a day by the airline industry. When you are listening to the flight attendants give the preflight instructions, invariably they instruct, "In the unlikely event that the cabin loses pressure, your oxygen mask will come down from the ceiling. Please pull it down fully, place it over your mouth and attach the string band around your ears." The next statement is very telling: "If traveling with small children, put your mask in place first, and then assist your child in placing his or her mask."

At first, that instruction flies in the face of a parent's conscience. Isn't it selfish to do for ourselves and put our child last? After all, we want the welfare of our child put before our own welfare. However, those instructions are intended to ensure that the parent is conscious and able to help the child. If the parent is incapacitated, then the child cannot survive.

As parents, we must attend first to our spiritual air masks. If we neglect the breath of God in our lives, then we will likely promote spiritual destruction in the lives of our children. I recently read this statement in *Home Life* magazine: "Take a deep breath of God's Spirit in your life, for your children are counting on it." As you have built your foundation, even so teach your child to pray, read the Bible, and recount the stories of Jesus and His forgiveness.

Make the Family a Priority

Making someone a priority always involves time and energy. As a parent, I have regrets in this area. I taught school in my children's formative years and missed some of their school plays, awards, field days, talent shows, concerts and special days. However, we cannot beat ourselves up over the past by saying, "If only I could do it over again." A poet wrote that the saddest words ever penned were "it might have been."

If you asked your children to name a great childhood memory, it will almost always be what a parent *did* for or with the child—never what the parent *gave* the child. Knowing this, parents and grandparents should make an effort to carve out quality time and invest in their children's lives. In Gloria Gaither's book *Let's Make a Memory*, she presents a host of creative ideas.

In spite of some of the regrets I feel, I know my three children grew up knowing they were a priority in my life. When my girls were young, we went camping in a pop-up camper all over the South and to Disney World every year. Money was tight, but we traveled every summer, making memories. They loved sleeping under the stars and eating pancakes, bacon and hot chocolate for breakfast.

To be honest, it was a sacrifice for me. My preschoolers loved the adventure, but I feared snakes! How I hated those midnight walks to the public rest rooms. But we made a memory and we sowed seed in their lives. My girls' love for camping continues to this day.

While at Samford University, our daughter Heather joined the spelunking club and actually spent the night in caves with bats and spiders! And when Kelli graduated from college, she didn't want a piece of jewelry. No! She wanted to receive money, borrow our car and trek out west, camping in national parks with her friends for three weeks! That is what camping did for my girls.

Establish traditions and special occasions that are celebrated and passed on. Holidays are an ideal time to focus on traditions.

It is important to support your children's interests. I fondly remember a trip I took with our son, Ronnie, to the SEC Championship Game in Atlanta. It meant missing a whole weekend of church, but the quality time with my son was priceless. We had a great time, and of course, the Crimson Tide won! We made every effort to never miss a football game or any other sport my son was involved in.

Building Traditions

Whether you are a mother, an aunt, a grandparent, or play some other nurturing role to a child, establish traditions and special occasions that are celebrated and passed on. Holidays are an ideal time to focus on traditions. I decorate for every holiday. I make a ridiculous bunny cake at Easter. When our children were teens, they disdained the bunny cake, but now the grandchildren love it. They help make it and help take it apart. It is easy to do, and it is exciting to continue a tradition that started when my girls were tiny.

Pray Over Your Children

From the cradle, children should hear Mom and Dad praying for them. Parents should learn to pray a blessing over their children. The Scripture teaches that the power of life and death is in the tongue (Proverbs 18:21). Speak and pour blessings over your children as Abraham did for his son, Isaac.

I recently saw a gripping television biography of Frank Sinatra. As his father was dying, Frank Sinatra told his father that he was a failure and wanted to quit music. His father told him, "Son, you are no quitter. I have always been so proud of you and your accomplishments."

After his father's death, Frank Sinatra's career catapulted into worldwide acclaim. I believe it was because of the blessing and assurance he received from his father.

Pray also for your child to know what sin is, and pray that each one will become a believer when he or she reaches the age of accountability. Ask God to protect your children and send angels to put a hedge of protection around them. I always prayed that God would keep me informed of everything that was going on in each child's life. Pray that your child will have a strong sense of righteousness. And it is never too early to pray that God would bring your children the right marriage partners.

Write down specific prayer requests for your children and grandchildren and then record the date these prayers are answered. Your fear as a parent will diminish, and your faith in the power of God will soar!

Let your babies hear you pray. Teach them to kneel and pray at a young age. Start with the blessing at meals and bedtime prayers. Read books of children's prayers. My daughters and I prayed each morning before the school bus came to pick them up for school.

When Kelli and Heather were preschoolers, someone gave us a puppy that grew into a big, ugly, lanky bird dog. At the end of his patience with this overgrown dog and amidst much protest, my husband finally hauled it off. With determined faith, every night my little girls prayed, "O God, bring our dog home!"

Within one week, one of our deacons showed up at the door, followed by a familiar-looking bird dog. He said, "Preacher, isn't this your dog?" Our girls learned volumes about God answering prayers, and Ron and I learned plenty too.

Teach children how to pray in daily, mundane life, and they will easily know how to pray in times of crisis. One Wednesday night after church, my young girls and I drove into our driveway, only to realize a robbery was taking place in our home. The three men broke two different doors as they fled with our treasures. We were unharmed, even though I ran through the house with a broom as a weapon! In the following months, fear gripped 6-year-old Heather. But through prayer, healing and sleep returned.

Pray for your children's classmates. Heather lost three teachers in death through car accidents and illness during her years in elementary and high school. We took each grief to the Lord in prayer together. We prayed through hurtful times, unfair situations and times of making difficult decisions.

When they were teenagers, I prayed that God would let my children be caught in every wrong action. God did just that. Remember this passage from Psalm 119:71, 72: "It is good for me that I have been afflicted, that I may learn Your statutes. The law of Your mouth is better to me." It is important to let your children experience the consequences of their actions, so that they might learn the wisdom of the Lord.

Train Your Child

Proverbs 22:6 states, "Train up a child in the way he should go, and when he is old he will not depart from it." Every child is different. Even Adam and Eve had different children. Cain had a bend toward agriculture, while Abel was good with handling flocks. Some children are strong-willed, and some are compliant. Some children need corporal punishment for correction, and others need just a stern look. Some are artistic, while others are analytical. Some are gregarious, others are timid. It is the parent's responsibility to find the way a child should go, and help prepare him or her in that way.

As you sit in the playroom of parenting and reflect on your work as a parent, please remember that your child will not do everything well. I made the mistake of wanting everything for my children. They cannot do sports, 4-H, scouts, art, ballet, music, and be top scholars all at the same time.

I encourage you to make a very short list of goals for your child, some that are general, and some that are lifelong. I would include a grateful heart as one goal. List the others as you learn more about your child, because differ-ent children will have different goals.

Every child should learn the Word of God and receive spiritual instruction from home first, and then from the church.

Psalm 112:1, 2 states, "Blessed is the man who fears the Lord, who delights greatly in His commandments. His descendants will be mighty on earth; the generation of the upright will be blessed."

Every child should learn the Word of God and receive spiritual instruction from home first, and then from the church. In 2 Timothy 3:15 Paul says of Timothy, "From childhood you have known the Holy Scriptures, which are able to make you wise for salvation through faith which is in Christ Jesus." A great milestone for me was to see my children repent and ask Jesus to be their Savior. When all three were baptized, it was such a balm to my heart to know that things were settled for eternity. One of the highlights of my life was on a trip to Israel, watching each of my children enter the empty Garden Tomb. Each child went into the tomb and came out moved to tears. I felt such a confirmation that their salvation was real.

As parents, we need to be real with our children. We need to be honest and consistent—a godly role model. Train up your children by example. In 1993, when Willie Nelson was 60 years old, he told his 23-year-old daughter, "Look at everything I do and do the opposite" (*Houston Chronicle,* May 1993). What an indictment. Contrast that attitude to Paul's words in 1 Corinthians 11:1, 2, "Imitate me, just as I also imitate Christ. Now I praise you, brethren, that you remember me in all things and keep the traditions just as I delivered them to you."

I remember a difficult time in Heather's life when we were at odds over everything. I wrote her every week while she was at college, but we are so much alike, we clashed. I did not approve of some things she was doing, and I told her so. One day we were on the back porch doing what we did best—arguing—when she pulled out a cigarette and started smoking. I got so mad, I yelled at her, "Give me a cigarette—I might as well join you!" Of course, I didn't smoke it, but she realized she was driving me to be irrational. Our laughter was great medicine and helped break the ice to more constructive discussion over our issues.

Give Love and Build Relationships

As I have shown from my own parenting examples, all is not a bed of roses in the playroom of parenting. A valuable lesson for parents to learn to say is, "I was wrong, please forgive me. I am so sorry." Scripture says to confess our faults one to another. As hard as it may be, that should include how we deal with our children.

Our children know our weaknesses, and they know we are not perfect. It is OK to quit pretending. We all fail and blow it from time to time. If we don't seek their forgiveness when we have wronged them, we will likely push them farther away from us.

Our children will not become our clones. They will always need our unconditional love. Noted author Gary Chapman has written a book titled *The Five Love Languages of Children* that every parent should read. He relates that children, like adults, have a basic way they hear love expressed the best: quality time, a gift of service, giving of gifts, physical affection or words of affirmation. Knowing your child's love language will enable you to communicate more effectively with him or her.

When a Child Fails

Where can children go for reassurance when they fail? I hope they can go to their parents. Parents should be ready to take the first step in reconciliation with their children. God took the first step to reconcile with us, His children.

In his poem, "Death of the Hired Man," Robert Frost said that home is the place you go where they *have* to take you in. The father's love of the Prodigal Son in the Gospels is a great example. In spite of the son's rebellious, irresponsible life, the father never stopped loving his child, longing and looking daily for his son's return. When at last he saw him return, the father welcomed his wayward child with open, loving arms. He did not judge or preach or give ultimatums. Instead, he lavished expensive presents on his rebellious son, giving him a robe, shoes, a ring and a party. What a welcome home!

We aren't told how the son reacted to this unconditional love, but we can imagine the great change that occurred in his life. The father no doubt forgave and forgot every trespass. A new and stronger bond between parent and child formed—one that would not be broken.

As parents, it is never too late to love and bless your children. This does not mean that you should take everything they dish out.

As parents, it is never too late to love and bless your children. This does not mean that you should take everything they dish out. There comes a time when they must take responsibility for their actions. Perhaps you have teenagers who are in rebellion and involved in destructive behaviors. No doubt your first instinct is to be angry, but what should be your role as a parent during such a difficult period?

First of all, be proactive! If you suspect drugs or alcohol, take them to be tested. Ask tough questions and persistently expect them to be accountable to you.

Next, bathe them in prayer. Let them know you are interceding and asking God to place a hedge of protection and correction around them. Prayer is a mighty spiritual weapon, and wielded in the life of a godly parent, the Enemy will falter!

Finally, be prepared to give ultimatums with tough

love. If your teens refuse to live by the rules you have set for your house, you may have to ask them to leave. That is surely the hardest step for the parent of a wayward teenager—to ask the child to pack up after you have spent years nurturing, protecting and providing for their needs. But when rebellion rules their spirit, you must be willing to "let go and let God," trusting the heavenly Father to deal with your child's heart.

Your act of tough love may be the beginning of a miracle road to restoration! While it is difficult to keep in mind that God loves our children more than we do, we must never forget He has a plan for their lives.

If you are sitting in the playroom of parenting, holding the broken pieces of a relationship with a rebellious or wayward child, kneel among those pieces and give them to God. In the study guide for this chapter, I included a list of promises I claimed over my son until God finished the chiseling on his character.

Enjoy the children God has placed in your life. The lessons we can learn from their innocence, their trials, their trust and their faith are sweet and valuable additions to our palette of life.

Review Questions

1. Recall a time as a child when your mother or father praised you or encouraged you. Tell how you felt.

2. Recount two of your fondest childhood memories with your family.

3. List traditions that are sacred in your home.

4. If you could have only five goals for your child, what would they be?

5. Briefly note how these scriptures influence parenting:
   Psalm 127:3-5

   Proverbs 17:6

   Proverbs 22:6

   Psalm 112:1, 2

   1 John 3:2

   1 Corinthians 13

6. Consider the following list to pray over your child:

ᔕ To come to know Christ as Savior (Psalm 63:1; 2 Timothy 3:15)

ᔕ Place a hedge of protection around them (Hosea 2:6)

ᔕ A respect for those in authority (Romans 13:1)

ᔕ Marry the right person (2 Corinthians 6:14-17)

ᔕ Resist Satan (James 4:7)

ᔕ Surround them with edifying friends (Proverbs 1:10, 11)

ᔕ Hold a hatred for sin (Psalm 97:10)

7. Read these scriptures and claim them for a wayward son or daughter:

Deuteronomy 20:4	Psalm 112:2-4
Psalm 78:7	Psalm 112:7
Psalm 50:3	Psalm 50:15
Psalm 51:10, 11	Psalm 51:17
Psalm 55:18	Psalm 55:22
Psalm 56:3, 4	Psalm 57:1-3
Psalm 62:5-8	Psalm 71:1-3

8. Consider each of your children/grandchildren. What are their primary love languages? Brainstorm 15 ways to say "I love you" to your child or grandchild.

9. Commit to pray the following blessings over your son or daughter:

For a Son:

May God make you as Ephraim and Manasseh, blessed and favored of God in all that you do. In the name of Jesus I say to you: "The Lord bless you and keep you; the Lord make His face shine upon you, and be gracious to you; the Lord lift up His countenance upon you, and give you peace" (Numbers 6:24-26). And I put on you today the name of God, and He shall bless you. Today I want you to know that your parents love you, and we are proud of you. I pray that you would have the heart of a father. I bless you with wisdom, courage, strength, character and integrity. I bless your understanding with enlightenment, that you may know what the will of God is for your life, your wife, your children and your children's children. I bless you with the favor of God and men on you all the days of your life as you walk in the paths of righteousness for His name's sake.

For a Daughter:

May God make you as Rachel and Leah, who built the house of Israel. Today, I want you to know that your parents love you, and we are proud of you. In the name of Jesus I say to you: "The Lord bless you and keep you; the Lord make His face shine upon you, and be gracious to you; the Lord lift up His countenance upon you, and give you peace" (Numbers 6:24-26). And I put on you today the name of God, and He shall bless you. I pray that you would have the heart of a mother. I bless you with virtue, purity, character and strength.

(Written by Ron Phillips and Sammy Wilson; used by permission)

As the marsh-hen secretly builds on the watery sod,
Behold I will build me a nest on the greatness of God:
I will fly in the greatness of God as the marsh-hen flies
In that freedom that fills all the space
'Twixt the marsh and the skies:
By so many roots as the marsh-grass sends in the sod
I will heartily lay me a-hold on the greatness of God:
Oh, like to the greatness of God is the greatness within
The range of the marshes, the liberal marshes of Glynn.

Lines 71-78
—Sidney Lanier, *Marshes of Glynn*

6

The Powder Room of Intimidation

he powder room is a place no one can avoid. In your house, you may call it the rest room, the bathroom, "the little girls room," or any variety of childhood nicknames; but inevitably, you will visit this room often during your day. We can avoid the living room for a time, or the back porch, or even the kitchen, but God made our bodies in such a way that we cannot avoid the powder room for long.

From the time we were little girls, the powder room offered us the glamour of mirrors. It is a rare woman who can pass a mirror without taking a good look. What do you see when you look in the mirror? Do you see a woman in need of a face-lift, new clothes, more exercise, a new figure, different hair color or new hairstyle, fewer wrinkles, more jewelry, or a youthful smile?

Of course, none of these things will give you strength of character, a positive self-esteem or the boldness in life that all women desire. Even knowing this, it seems we are never satisfied with the image staring back at us each day from the mirror. For some women, that image is distorted, discontented, dissatisfied or unappreciated. For others, seeing the image creates a sense of fear—fear of aging, fear of the future, fear of the past, and fear of the opinions of others.

The image we have of ourselves affects our total well-being. But that image is going to change . . .

It comes down to this: The image we have of ourselves affects our total well-being. But that image is going to change—there is no fountain of youth, and time keeps marching on. So, if our image is sure to change, then we must confront what lies at the root of our lack of significance.

A Woman's Enemy

Intimidation is a force or spirit all people confront, especially women. The word *intimidation* means "the act of making one afraid." To intimidate is to influence or force to fear. When this fear is forced on us, it unleashes a storm of trouble in the form of . . .

♈ Discouragement

♈ Confusion and frustration over goals and dreams

♈ Loss of direction and a belief that everything is impossible

♈ Lack of self-confidence, self-image, power to succeed and ability to confront.

It also . . .

෴ Causes you to do things you don't want to do

෴ Causes you to back off from what God has desired for you

෴ Leads you to compromise and tolerate what is offensive

෴ Creates fear that your past will become your future and will be horrible, unsafe or deadly.

This spirit of intimidation can paralyze you. What intimidates you?

In the ninth grade, I had a teacher who, with one word or look, could cause me to forget my name, along with all the material I had studied for a test! This small, wiry, middle-aged English teacher was the wife of a Methodist minister. She was intimidation personified. I loved the subject matter, but I feared her wrath.

One day when I forgot to have my parents sign a paper, she required me to stay after school. Unfortunately, I completely forgot. By the time I realized what I had done, supper was over, and I couldn't sleep all that night worrying about the inevitable.

Trying desperately to make amends, I arrived at her room early the next morning. I apologized and told the truth, volunteering to stay after school that day. This woman looked me square in the face and said, "Young lady, I ought to cut your throat and watch the blood run." My eyes bulged, my mouth flew open, and I almost fainted. She let me "stew" for about a minute before she burst out laughing at my reaction. She let me off the hook that time, but I have never forgotten how she made me feel. It certainly was not a joke to me.

We tend to be intimidated by people who are in authority, people we want to impress, and people we love. The Bible exposes this spirit of intimidation and teaches us how to defeat it. No matter how pleasant our personality is, how positive our attitude is, and how smart we are, we will never defeat it. But we can overcome it with the Word of God.

Yielding to Intimidation

In this postmodern age, many homes reveal a tragic scene: children who intimidate their parents. I have watched parents of 2-year-olds giving their God-given authority over to their child. Parents cajole, pamper, pacify, negotiate and even wring their hands. The child's behavior already reveals that they have no boundaries. As a high school English teacher for 20 years, I knew teens who despised and threatened their parents blatantly. Worse yet, I watched the parents' reaction: a shy smile and a shrug of the shoulders as if to say, "What are kids coming to today?"

The Bible gives us instruction about this exact issue in 1 Samuel 2 and 3. "And the word of the Lord was rare in those days; there was no widespread revelation" (3:1). This verse doesn't refer to the written Word of God, because they did have the books of Moses, but they did not have dreams, visions, insights and fresh revelation from God. They did not have the glory cloud by day, the fire by night or the cloud covering the Tabernacle. God's intervention in their lives was a distant memory—a story told by grandparents to grandchildren. God was silent. And there was a reason.

Their prophet, priest and judge was Eli, a man intimidated by his own sons. Eli was the seventh high priest of Israel. For 40 years, he had loved and served God. He was not a novice or a new believer; he was a seasoned veteran of faith. Eli was God's representative—the head of state. He was the voice of God to the people; yet Eli didn't finish well.

In 1 Samuel 2:22, Hophni and Phinehas, Eli's sons, were operating as priests, but they were wicked, corrupt men—fornicating with the women of Israel even in the Tabernacle of God. Without respect or reverence for God or their father, they took by force the meat the people brought for sacrificing, making the people dread their trips to the Tabernacle. These unlawful sons despised and desecrated what was holy. Eli was their father, their employer, head of church and head of state (judge); yet they had no respect for him or God.

All Eli did in response was to give them a little slap on the wrist—a mild rebuke. Scripture says, "He heard everything his sons did to all Israel. So he said to them, 'Why do you do such things? For I hear of your evil dealings from all the people. No, my sons! For it is not a good report that I hear. You make the Lord's people transgress" (vv. 22-24).

Eli should have delivered a strong correction, removed them from office, and punished them. But he did nothing! In verse 29, a man of God confronted Eli and exposed the spirit of intimidation: "Why do you kick at My sacrifice and offering which I have commanded in My dwelling place, and honor your sons more than Me, to make yourselves fat with the best of all the offerings of Israel My people?"

In the end, Eli revered his sons more than he respected his God. His judgment and death is prophesied in verse 30. In verses 31-34 the sudden early deaths of his sons are prophesied. Matthew 10:37 states, "He who loves father or mother more than Me is not worthy of Me. And he who loves son or daughter more than Me is not worthy of Me."

Once again, what intimidates you? When you give up your God-given authority, everyone under you suffers. When Eli gave control to his sons, he lost his own authority, he lost his ability to judge the people, and he lost his relationship with God. The reason the nation had no direct revelation of God during Eli's years in power was because of his lack of spiritual leadership. Compromise is costly.

The apostle Paul found himself in a very imposing situation in Acts 25 and 26. Called before the great King Agrippa, Paul made a choice: In spite of intimidation all around, he boldly spoke forth the gospel.

Unfortunately, King Agrippa was more sensitive to the influences of intimidation. In Acts 26:28, King Agrippa confesses to Paul, "You almost persuaded me to become a Christian." I contend that this powerful man could not become a Christian because he worried about what people would think of him. His pride would not allow him to humble himself before his influential court and pray for the forgiveness of his sins. He yielded to the fear of man. *Almost* is an ugly word . . . a negative word . . . a defeated word. His intimidation cost him eternal life. Almost is *never* enough.

Proverbs 29:25 states, "The fear of man brings a snare, but whoever trusts in the Lord shall be safe."

Standing Against Intimidation

When Ron and I had been married less than a year, he preached a revival in a small Baptist church not far from our church. During the middle of his sermon on hell, fire and judgment, a man three times his age screamed from the back of the church, "That's a lie! Don't believe him!"

My 21-year-old, inexperienced husband could have yielded to that intimidation, but he did not. He stood on the authority as a messenger of the Word of God. He stood tall behind that pulpit and firmly rebuked the man, saying, "This is not a lie, it is the true and living Word of God. You, sir, will sit down and shut up." My husband took back the control of that service on the authority of the Bible. Second Timothy 1:7 states, "God has not given us a spirit of fear, but of power and of love and of a sound mind."

No matter what intimidates you—your mate, your boss, your parent, your friends, your pastor, the church elders, or just fear itself—you should know it is understandable to be afraid. But don't yield to it. Ralph Waldo Emerson, the great American poet and essayist, said, "Do the thing you fear and the fear leaves you." In other words, confront your fear. Deal with it, and you will defeat it. Isaiah 54:17 states, "No weapon formed against you shall prosper, and every tongue which rises against you in judgment you shall condemn. This is the heritage of the servants of the Lord."

The last half of that verse means that you should verbally condemn the actions of those that speak intimidation over you. The words *you can't* or *you're not*, put up a warning flag, These are phrases of intimidation. When someone tries to tell you you're not trained enough, you're not talented enough, you're not smart enough . . . stand firm without fear and state: "I can do all things through Christ who strengthens me" (Philippians 4:13).

In the gripping movie *As Good As It Gets*, starring Jack Nicholson and Helen Hunt, we have a reality check about two fearful people who are intimidated. Helen Hunt plays a waitress who lives in poverty as a single mother. Responsible for her mother and severely asthmatic son, she is intimidated and beaten down by the harsh circumstances of life.

Jack Nicholson plays the role of a successful and rich misfit of a writer. He is reclusive, insulting, prejudiced, odd and mean-spirited. His many quirks include refusing to allow anyone in his home, resisting any kind of change, and having obsessive compulsive behaviors, such as eating the same meal every day in the same restaurant with his own plastic utensils. He is a clean freak and will not walk on cracks in sidewalks.

At the end of the movie, these two needy people become friends. In the last five minutes, as the two characters share a caress and walk away in the darkness, you notice that Nicholson's character no longer worries about avoiding the cracks in the sidewalk. What a perfect example of the scripture, "Perfect love casts out fear."

Living in Freedom

When we do not live in fear, we have victory and success in our lives. Boldness takes over and along with it comes self-confidence. We become proactive, interactive, offensive and aggressive. Scripture tells us, "You shall receive power when the Holy Spirit has come upon you" (Acts 1:8).

> *When we do not live in fear, we have victory and success in our lives. Boldness takes over and along with it comes self-confidence.*

Do you have the boldness of David, ready to fight the giants in your life? In 1 Samuel 17, young David could have easily been intimidated by Goliath, but he didn't yield. When David arrived near the battlefield to deliver supplies to his brothers, he heard the bellowing threats and curses from Goliath. He asked why someone didn't "take out" the loud-mouthed Philistine who was defiling God's name and the armies of Israel. Frustrated at the cowardice around him, David offered to fight the giant.

In verse 28, David's brother tries to intimidate him. Eliab may have been jealous of David, because he and all David's other brothers had been present years before when Samuel anointed David king. Eliab was embarrassed that his younger brother was showing all the rest of them up as cowards, so Eliab tried to put David back in his place as a lowly shepherd of a few sheep—an insolent and prideful boy caught up in the glory of war.

He said in essence, "David, who do you think you are, coming here and bragging like that?"

King Saul also tried to intimidate David with his heavy armor. I am sure the king was convicted of his own cowardice in allowing a youth to become involved in a fight that should have been his.

Goliath himself tried to intimidate David. He disdained him because David was young. He said, "Am I a dog, that you come to me with sticks?" (v. 43). He cursed David and made fun of him. But David boldly yelled to Goliath, "I come to you in the name of the Lord of Hosts" (v. 45). David was the victor. He did everything to Goliath that Goliath had threatened to do to him.

It is time for you to claim victory over the intimidation in your life. Parents, take back your authority over your children. You are in charge; you make the rules and standards. You enforce the law in your home. You are the adult, the mature one. Don't give in to lesser things. Be bold. Be on the offensive, not the defensive.

If you find yourself staring in the mirror of the powder room of intimidation and feel yourself struggling for victory, pray this prayer boldly:

In the name of the Lord Jesus Christ and through the blood of Jesus, I speak to the spirit of fear that has controlled me in the past. I renounce all words of intimidation spoken over me by other people and break that power over me. I count null and void all words of intimidation I have spoken over myself. I take authority over all the spirits of fear. I reject you in the name of Jesus, and command you to leave me and never return. I give you no place in my life, and I bind you and command you to leave now, because my body is the temple of the living God and I submit to God alone. I exercise my faith. I know I am saved, I am blessed with all the blessings of Abraham, and what God has blessed will never be cursed with intimidation or fear. Amen.

Review Questions

1. Name three women you admire and tell three qualities that make them special.

2. If someone put you on that list, what qualities would others see in you? What do you see in yourself when you look in the powder-room mirror?

3. Define *intimidation* as discussed in this chapter.

4. Intimidation is a spirit. List four people or things that often intimidate us:

   a.

   b.

   c.

   d.

5. By whom was the priest Eli intimidated, and what did it cost him?

6. Name the three sources of intimidation David faced in 1 Samuel 17:26, 28.

7. Read Acts 25:23 and 26:27-29. Into what intimidating situation was Paul placed, and what was the result?

8. How do each of these scriptures address the subject of intimidation?

   Joshua 1:9

   Psalm 119:37

   John 14:27

   Psalm 84:12

9. List times in your life when you were intimidated. Remember times when God gave you victory over intimidation.

"And above all things have fervent love for
one another, for "love will cover a multitude of sins."
Be hospitable to one another without grumbling.
As each one has received a gift, minister it to one
another, as good stewards of the manifold
grace of God"
(1 Peter 4:8-10).

7

The Kitchen of Hospitality

I'm sure some of my readers have been looking forward to this chapter. You know who you are—you love your kitchen, and you are master of this part of your heart and home. You enjoy the whole experience of cooking, baking, and sharing your domestic skills with friends and family. Whether your cabinets and drawers abound with the latest kitchen gadgets or have only a well-worn set of kitchen knives and wire whisks, you find joy in the moments spent in creative homemaking.

However, you may be a woman who prefers to run from the kitchen. Piles of cookbooks and hospitality magazines haven't inspired you. You dread cooking, and you refuse to master this room.

When was the last time you entertained in your home? Now dig even deeper . . . when was the last time you hosted someone in your home other than your family or your very best friends? Even though your intentions are good, time gets away from you, and you soon realize the halls haven't echoed with fellowship and fun in a long while. It is time to change that. Set a goal for entertaining and go for it! There is no wrong motive for hospitality in our homes.

Satan loves to isolate women in their homes. Our Enemy knows hospitality is a powerful ministry to others. It holds many rewards. Luke 10:40 tells us how Martha ministered to the human needs of our Lord Jesus while He was on earth. She served and prepared food for Jesus and other guests. She gave all of her energy to be sure that she was a good hostess and that the table was filled with food when He was in her home. Sometimes before we can minister to the spiritual needs of others, we must minister to their physical needs first.

Sometimes before we can minister to the spiritual needs of others, we must minister to their physical needs first.

Training to Serve

Hospitality can be learned. You can be hospitable without breaking the bank. You don't have to serve T-bone steaks every time you entertain. Chili, spaghetti or burgers make great suppers. Don't wear yourself out in an attempt to impress those you are serving. Stress, fatigue and exhaustion may cause you to throw up your hands and never try to entertain again.

One of my most memorable meals was years ago at a church member's home after Sunday night worship. This home was very casual, but cheerful. The kitchen was decorated in bright red. Our hostess served a simple, but delicious, bean soup. It is strange that I remember all about that evening, and nothing about so many others. I learned from that evening that it doesn't matter what food you have, what matters is how you treat people. We all had a good time, and as far as we could tell, there was no stress.

For many years, Ron and I hosted an open house at Christmas for our entire church family on Sunday afternoon or Saturday night. I would serve punch, coffee and cakes as people dropped by for a few minutes of chatting. The church people loved coming to their pastor's home. I did not fully realize at first what a sense of friendship and bonding this accomplished with our people.

Another event for which we opened our home regularly was a graduation luncheon for our high school seniors. We would empty our basement of all furniture, cover tables with paper cloths, and adorn the walls with high school jerseys, pom-poms and banners. Some years we fed up to 50 students. What fun we had, with no program or agenda.

Our Inspiration for Hospitality

The Bible is our inspiration for every part of our lives, including hospitality. Abraham is the first Biblical example of hospitality we read about in Genesis 18:1-8. In this account, three men (who were likely angels) appeared to Abraham and agreed to stay for supper. Sarah made bread cakes and their servant prepared a calf. Abraham gave the men bread, meat, butter and milk to eat. Abraham and

Sarah didn't expect anything in return for their hospitality, but by the time the men had left, God had delivered a promise to them that they would have a son.

The Bible commands us to meet the physical needs of people. Proverbs 18:24 tells us, "A man who has friends must himself be friendly." This is sometimes inconvenient, because friends often seem to need you at the most inopportune time. To be a friend is an investment of time, energy and money, but the investment is eternal.

To be a friend is an investment of time, energy and money, but the investment is eternal.

One of the most powerful passages on hospitality is found in Matthew 25:40, when Jesus said, "Inasmuch as you did it to one of the least of these My brethren, you did it to Me." Jesus revealed that anytime we feed the hungry, give water in His name, take in a stranger, give clothes to the needy or visit prisoners, it is like we are doing it for Jesus himself! The Scripture says, "To him who knows to do good and does not do it, to him it is sin" (James 4:17).

I fear that much of the time we get so stressed, upset and frazzled that we yell at the family and kick the dog! Do you get so uptight that you blow up at the family and then wish the company wouldn't come? Relax. Unwind. Slow down. No one will remember what you served. They don't care if there is dust under the bed. Light candles, and the dust won't show. We don't have to be perfect. Enjoy your guests, calm down and make memories with friends.

The Perfect Host

Our Lord knew how to make guests feel comfortable, welcome and at ease. In John 21, Jesus called to the disciples fishing and said, "Children, have you any food?" He then said, "Cast the net on the right side . . . and bring some of the fish which you have just caught" (vv. 5, 6, 12). This was after the Resurrection, and Jesus cooked breakfast for the disciples on the seashore. He told them to come and dine. Our Lord taught by example.

When you prepare for guests, do your best and then enter His rest. If you are worried about performing well, you will never enjoy your company. One day our Lord will cook for us also. He will prepare the Marriage Supper of the Lamb, where He will be our host and we will be the honored guests. That will be the greatest celebration ever.

Titus 1:8 says be a "lover of hospitality" (KJV). This attitude, of course, begins in the heart. Do you know your neighbors? You probably know only two or three families in your neighborhood. Get started!

We learn so much around the dinner table. As we talk, we feel peace and acceptance. We learn to recognize truth and iron things out. We banter back and forth until we draw conclusions and learn to compromise. We mold character at the dinner table, and we share our lives, emotions, philosophies, knowledge and convictions. We make memories and forge friendships.

Looking back over all the guests we've had in our home—from millionaires to the homeless—I will say without a doubt the most honored guest ever in my home was Baker James Cauthern. Growing up as a little

Baptist girl, I learned that Baker James Cauthern was the "Man." He was a foreign missionary to China and executive secretary to our denomination's Mission Board. How honored we were to have him speak at a mission banquet at our church and share a meal in our home.

Prior to his coming, we read his autobiography and learned everything we could about him. He was the most charming and well-mannered guest we ever welcomed. He honored my children by answering every question and giving them his full attention. How we all loved him! He had eaten in the finest places in the world, but he complimented me on the meal. How glad I was that we opened our home to him. I could have missed that whole experience if I had refused to serve him because of my shyness or lack of confidence. We did not know that three months later he would be in heaven.

Motivated to Entertain

There is no wrong reason for hospitality. Some people enjoy hospitality because they want to avoid loneliness. With our busyness and lack of intimacy with others, we want a deeper level of friendship. That is a good motive for hospitality.

Sometimes people want to show off. I heard about a woman who bought all new bedspreads for a party she was having in her home. The next day, she took all the bedspreads back. You really cannot have fun until you get comfortable with your boundaries. Live with the worn-out carpets, curtainless windows and know you will have burned food sometimes. For a gracious hostess, none of these things will matter, as long as her guests are treated with love and respect.

Spur-of-the-moment entertaining is perhaps the best kind, because we can serve hot dogs or chili. We can say, "Come over for dessert or watermelon," or "We're going to order pizza, come on over just to sit and talk." This type of entertaining doesn't involve preparation or stress, but it goes a long way to feed the soul.

Spur-of-the-moment entertaining is perhaps the best kind, because we can serve hot dogs or chili.

Yet another motivation to entertaining is an upcoming holiday such as Christmas, Easter, Fourth of July, weddings or birthdays, graduations or baby dedications. Master a special menu, and feature that menu for a festive day each year. Traditions will help you finalize all the details.

Some people entertain to advance their careers or to impress their boss. Wanting a promotion is not a bad thing, but you must focus on making the boss feel comfortable and welcome in your home. A gracious, hospitable family will be an asset to any corporation or ministry.

Sad times are also times of hospitality. Wakes and funerals are times of comfort and strength for the hurting. Invariably someone says, "Do you remember when . . ." Then the good times come back to mind, making the sad times more tolerable.

Prepare a Heart of Hospitality

Your only drawback to hospitality is your own negative self-image. Only you can make yourself feel guilty. One way to prepare for entertaining is to know that disasters will come. At least one small disaster will happen every time! There will be the times where you will forget to put sugar in the whipping cream, as I did once!

When I was newly married, I did not know much about cooking. I could make barbecue chicken and spaghetti, and that was about it! Over time, I learned new skills in the kitchen and grew as a hostess, especially for my family and also for those we invited to our home.

When you entertain, count on the fact that someone will spill something or break a dish. A candle may set the tablecloth on fire. The candle wax may drip on the mantle. Your picnic will be rained out or the electricity will go off. Don't let little annoyances paralyze you. If you laugh, your guests will too.

The last time I had our whole church staff for dinner, we fed around 40 people with every downstairs room in my home filled with tables. I put tables in the den and in the dining room. That particular Christmas I served beef Wellington. I like it, and I thought Ron would like it. When he took one bite he said, "What is in this meat?" When I said "Liver pâté," he almost spit it across the room! Now it is a joke we share with our staff, anytime beef Wellington is mentioned, or anytime we see it on the menu somewhere.

Remember Jesus went about doing good. Get organized and avoid tension. Learn the skills needed for entertaining.

Determine your purpose and begin setting your goals. Do not go shopping and buy things just for the party. The Scripture says everything should be done decently and in order. Prepare things ahead of time. This applies to your hospitality to your family as well as to your guests.

Take Charge

Here are a few tips that may help you transform your kitchen into a center of Christian love and hospitality:

- ♥ Consider designating a "cooking day." Plan a week of meals and put some in the freezer.

- ♥ Cook enough to share with others (especially sweets like banana nut bread, cakes or muffins).

- ♥ Keep a few great menus. When your family enjoys a new dish, consider preparing it for a special occasion.

- ♥ Don't overload your week—attempt only one new project per week.

- ♥ Make lists! It is frustrating to be in the middle of a recipe only to find you are missing a key ingredient!

- ♥ Let your guests help!

- ♥ Teach your children to cook, encouraging them to clean as they go along.

- ♥ Have routines that you follow morning and night, to keep your home clean and ready for use.

- ♥ When doing that final cleanup before a party, carry

a plastic caddy of cleaning supplies to each room and a trash bag. If something isn't dirty, don't clean it!

♡ Don't be a martyr and do it all if you are pressed for time. Use shortcuts—buy salads at deli, buy desserts, order out.

♡ Have an emergency shelf with a few tried-and-true quick recipes for when company shows up unexpectedly. When you serve it with love and care, even a boxed mix can say, "Welcome to my home; I'm glad you're here!"

♡ Treat your family as honored guests for meals. Set the table beautifully. Add flowers or candles so that your family feels special. Hospitality begins with those you love the most.

♡ Before people leave your home, pray a prayer of friendship and blessings in their life. This too will draw you together.

Review Questions

1. Why do you think women today are not more hospitable?

2. Here are several Scriptural inspirations for hospitality; think about how each one can help you personally:

   Genesis 18:1-8

   Proverbs 18:24

   Matthew 25:40

   John 21:5-12

   Romans 12:13

   Hebrews 13:2

   1 Peter 4:9

   Titus 1:8

3. List the basic motivations for hospitality.

4. Recall some of the disasters you had when entertaining that you can now laugh about. Write one of them below.

5. Do a critical inventory of your food-shopping habits. What are some ways you could improve?

6. Give an example of when you experienced a rewarding time of hospitality.

Friendship

Ministry Traditions

Memories

Comfort

Celebration

Creativity

"God is God. Because He is God,
He is worthy of my trust and obedience.
I will find rest nowhere but in His holy will,
a will that is unspeakably beyond
my largest notions of what He is up to."

—Elisabeth Elliot
Through Gates of Splendor

8

The Guest Room of Rest

In the guest room of our homes, company should be encouraged to rest. If you have a spare bedroom that has been abandoned by a son or daughter who is off to college or who has married, you have the ideal chance to open your home for out-of-town guests.

Even though we know this room should be peaceful, calm and restful, too often it is filled with leftovers and a hodgepodge of whatever is extra in our home. Or even worse, it becomes the "catch-all" room—piled with assorted sewing projects, old magazines you've never read, and bags of clothes and other items you intend to take to charity. If someone needs to spend the night at your home, you're not even sure you could find the bed in that room.

A lack of rest and sleep robs us of the strength and energy our bodies desperately require. You can make physical changes in a room that can promote this rest.

Think about how you would tackle the remaking of a guest room. The decor of this room must be deliberate and well-planned. This room cannot become a landing zone for unwanted or dilapidated hand-me-down furniture. Restful colors or wallpaper should welcome the visitor. A comfortable, overstuffed chair and ottoman, along with reading materials, a lamp and table, will indicate that it is a place for taking a break. Flowers, candles, a table fountain, chocolates, prepackaged snacks and bottled water on an attractive tray can satisfy late-night hunger. Other amenities in the room could include fluffy towels, bath products, music and space in the closet for clothes. A must for any guest room is a Bible, a note pad, and pen or pencil.

True rest involves the condition of your soul. How can I have this calming, tranquil inner Sabbath?

However, an inviting room is not the only answer to the quest for rest. Rest for the physical body is not enough; we must have rest for our souls. In Matthew 11:28-30, Jesus promised precisely that.

"Come to Me, all you who labor and are heavy laden, and I will give you rest. Take My yoke upon you and learn from Me, for I am gentle and lowly in heart, and you will find rest for your souls. For My yoke is easy and My burden is light."

The Secret of Rest
True rest involves the condition of your soul. How can

I have this calming, tranquil inner Sabbath? Scripture uses the words *rest* and *Sabbath* interchangeably, but both words may translate "stop, end or cease." In Genesis 2:1-3 when God finished His creative work, He stopped from all His work on the seventh day and called the Sabbath day a day of rest—a holy day, a sanctified day of rest and restoration. God himself rested because He had completed His work.

Stopping is beneficial for our physical well-being and for our optimum performance. We must recharge our physical bodies just as we recharge a battery, for our good.

However, just as our physical bodies need rest, our "soul" must rest in the Lord, who is our peace and our rest. The Scriptures teach, "Be still, and know that I am God" (Psalm 46:10). How do we rest? Delight in our God. Enjoy God's presence and promises. Press the "pause button" in your life. Celebrate Jesus with thankful words and praise. Give God the pleasure of your company. You will have times of refreshing. You will feel as if you are standing under a gentle waterfall and are being washed from head to toe. Jesus said "learn from Me" (Matthew 11:29); and in these quiet Sabbaths you can rest in worship, praise and prayer, and He will "show you great and mighty things which you do not know" (Jeremiah 33:3).

Rest: A Continuing Need

Few things in life are more priceless than a good night's sleep! If you agree with this statement, you are among those who are crying out for true rest. A recent study by the National Commission of Sleep Disorders showed that America shoulders at least $15.9 billion each year as the direct cost of sleep deprivation on our culture, with an estimated $50 to $100 billion in indirect and related costs. So much is spent in the search for elusive sleep, and yet fatigue takes its toll.

Young children often have trouble sleeping. Some are plagued with nightmares and stress. Elementary and high school girls are tortured with the demands of school, competitions, recreation and too many commitments. The insecurity of an unstable home adds to the burden of sleeplessness.

The cycle continues in college students, who burn the proverbial candle at both ends, causing fatigue and lack of rest. Although they appear focused and "together," they adopt a lifestyle of all-night cramming sessions (with the aid of caffeine boosters) and a whirlwind social schedule.

Young mothers are no exception to the sleep famine. They must nurture newborn babies who have their days and nights reversed, and sick children who demand around-the-clock attention, causing moms to be sleep-deprived, irritable and barely able to function. With so many demands on their time, young mothers rarely schedule time to rest and recover.

Career women also reflect this lack-of-rest lifestyle, thinking that they must perform tasks quicker and better than anyone else. Climbing the ladder of success is demanding, and promotion becomes a cruel taskmaster as they try to be it all, invent it all, achieve it all, conquer it all and have it all.

As women enter the menopausal years, they suffer from diminishing hormones, which cause imbalances and insomnia. Rest cannot be found. Pills are addictive and offer only a temporary solution.

When opportunities for rest become available, many women are unsure how to capture those moments. It is sobering to realize that too many of us have become people of extremes who lack balance and rest.

However, there is hope for the weary woman. Christian women can know true rest in the resources provided by the Holy Spirit.

One-on-one time with God, in the quietness of your home, allows you to focus on the things of God without interruption.

Rest From the Father

I had the privilege of assisting my husband with a chapter in his book *Awakened by the Spirit*. I did an expansive study of what the Bible says about rest and was overwhelmed with what I found. Some of the material that follows is taken from that chapter.

You can seek a rest experience with God at home, in intimate fellowship with Him. One-on-one time with God, in the quietness of your home, allows you to focus on the things of God without interruption, whether it be in your favorite nook, desk table or back-porch swing. As you read the Scripture, you can reflect on God's work in your life, remind Him in prayer of your hurts and needs, repent of any sin, and find that this removes all obstacles from knowing Him intimately.

In this special rendezvous with God, we can be

genuine and pour out our soul, emptying ourselves of selfishness, pride and problems. God comforts us like a soft, warm blanket to assure us, encourage us and love us. A result of these quiet times is rest in the midst of a busy day. You can find peace in every task and a quiet confidence to know God cares about every detail of your life. As you function in His presence, you will find that, amazingly, the hours in the day will seem to multiply, and tasks will fall supernaturally into place.

You can also find rest at church when you worship and praise the Father. The Scriptures teach that the Lord inhabits the praises of His people. God delights when you sing, testify and bless His name. When you enter into His presence, you may cry, pray, move, dance, shout, clap, or listen to His still, small voice. Regardless of your method of expression, you draw near to the heart of God when you worship, and life's cares drift away, becoming insignificant when compared to God's eternal plan. That brings rest.

At other times, God chooses to bring rest to us through prayer and the laying on of hands, sometimes resulting in "being slain in the Spirit" or what some call "falling out." This supernatural touch from God is a powerful visitation of rest that has well-established Biblical roots, as I discovered after such an experience in my own life several years ago.

Heavenly Time-Out

In 1997, I invited the anointed soloist Judy Jacobs to sing and speak at our "Ladies Night Out"—a special women's gathering we plan each year. Six months prior to the meeting, over 50 leaders in our Women's Council began preparing for that special night, praying for God to grant a new level of anointing and ministry to women. We prayed for a "new thing." We prayed boldly and daily.

God gave us a special prayer promise in Matthew 11:12: "The kingdom of heaven suffers violence, and the violent take it back by force." We claimed that verse for weary and hurting women. We believed God was asking us to become militant in taking spiritual authority over our children, our homes, and our futures, and in claiming our deliverance.

That night over 500 women were present as Judy Jacobs stood to sing and preach. To our amazement, she called out her Scripture text for the night: Matthew 11:12, our prayer promise verse! An air of expectation filled the house, and we sat expecting God to move.

God's presence was real, and His deliverance was powerful. Over half of the women in attendance gathered on the stage and around the podium for prayer that night. Hurting hearts were mended, and the promises of God were claimed on behalf of erring children, torn marriages and desperate situations.

As the mistress of ceremonies, I was preparing to close the worship service when suddenly Judy took the microphone. Without touching me in any way, she began to prophesy over me, and I fell to the floor in front of 500 women. No one was there to catch me; God simply let me down gently.

It is important to note that this had never happened to me before. I was "Baptist-born" and "Baptist-wed." I had been a Baptist preacher's wife for almost 30 years and considered myself a very unlikely candidate for that type of experience. My background as a teacher, a classical musician and a reserved Southern lady assured me that I would never make a spectacle of myself. However, on this special night, I was slain in the Spirit and fell immobile under the heaviness of God.

Why did God do that to me publicly? He may have had many reasons. First, I can tell you that freedom broke over me that night. The ropes and chains of tradition, which for years had held me bound to guilt, legalistic rules and religious traditions, fell off.

Just as importantly, God caused me to lie down in green pastures. He restored my soul (Psalm 23). I was overwhelmed with great peace and joy. When I came up from that restful trance, I knew undeniably that the Lord had done a great thing for me, and I was so very glad.

Among the many results of that night was the breaking of my pride before the women I served, and a new ministry being spoken over me. When I was praying that God would do a new thing for women on that night, I had no idea He would choose to do a public work through me. I experienced a personal revival, a deeper thirst for God, a greater confidence in God's power and a fresh release for ministry. A militant faith rose inside me. I became more aware that "I can do all things through Christ who strengthens me" (Philippians 4:13). Am I better for this? The answer is a resounding "yes!"

I began an honest study of the Holy Scriptures, and found that rest is a part of God's supernatural visitation to man. In describing their experiences, people will often say that they are still conscious, yet totally engaged with the Lord.

Significant changes occur in your life when God visits you with His rest and peace. No matter what kind of rest God chooses to minister to you, a number of different results may occur.

1. *Heavenly Emergency Room.* Sometimes during a God-given rest period, He may provide healing for you in a spiritual, emotional, mental or physical way. In Genesis 2:21, God caused a "deep sleep" to fall on Adam so He could remove a rib in order to fashion woman. He performed this surgery while Adam slept. He not only removed the rib, but also healed Adam's body after the surgery. Adam felt God's touch on his life in his physical body.

At a camp meeting in Tennessee, a 9-year-old boy came to the altar for prayer. He was "slain in the Spirit" and remained on the floor until after my husband and I left the auditorium with the host pastor. In a few moments, we heard a great shout arise from the auditorium. In moments, we learned that the young boy had arisen from the floor healed of an eye problem that two surgeries had not been able to correct!

2. *A Clear Vision of the Path Ahead.* Another example of God's ministry of rest is in Genesis 15:12, where God put Abram in a deep sleep. God then prophesied, or spoke the future over Abram's spirit. God promised that Abram would live to a good old age. Abram listened in his trance and heard the voice of God.

The prophet Ezekiel also had several experiences where God visited him in a trance. Ezekiel 2:2 records one occurrence when the prophet saw a vision and heard a voice. He was commissioned to a new ministry.

Ezekiel wasn't the only Biblical figure to have the Spirit of God overpower him. During a rest experience, Daniel heard the voice of an angel speaking about the end of time. When the trance was over, Daniel fainted and was sick for days (Daniel 8:27). And in Acts 10:10, the apostle Peter had an encounter as he prayed alone on a rooftop. In an electrifying vision, God called Peter into a new ministry to the Gentiles.

God causes a season of rest to confront us with the need for change and repentance in our lives.

3. *A Fresh Awareness of the Divine.* Often God may visit us to give us a new sense of His power and glory. In our fast pace of living, we often lose our vision of the greatness of the Lord. Matthew 17:6 tells of the disciples' experience at the Transfiguration. On that mountain, God showed Jesus' followers the significance of the Law and Prophets, and that Jesus was greater and the fulfillment of both. When the disciples heard this, they fell to the ground with their faces down. A touch from Jesus reassured them gently.

The whole Book of Revelation is a vision of God's glory to the beloved apostle John. In 1:10, John described his encounter: "I was in the Spirit on the Lord's Day, and I heard behind me a loud voice, as of a trumpet." Verse 17 tells us more: "And when I saw Him, I fell at His feet as dead. But He laid His right hand on me, saying to me, 'Do not be afraid; I am the First and the Last.'"

John saw many things in the vision and heard the voice of Jesus. He was a witness to the Word of God and to the testimony of Jesus. He saw, heard and obeyed a heavenly vision after spending time with his Father.

4. *Correction and Regeneration.* Finally, God causes a season of rest to confront us with the need for change and repentance in our lives. The Book of Acts tells of Paul's conversion on the road to Damascus. With papers in hand to arrest and kill more Christians, a bright light from heaven appeared and seized him. He fell to the ground blinded, and then he heard a voice from heaven. The Lord revealed Himself to him in power, saying, "I am Jesus, whom you are persecuting" (9:5).

When Paul arose from that experience, he was blind for several days. Although his physical sight was temporarily gone, his spiritual eyes could see clearly. In a trance, he received confrontation and correction from Jesus.

In Numbers 24, we read where God used a mercenary false prophet, a mere magician and sorcerer, to speak the word of God. A king had paid Balaam the sorcerer to curse the people of God, but each attempt would end with him falling down with his eyes wide open, seeing a vision from Almighty God. Instead of curses, *blessings* for the nation of Israel came forth from his mouth.

The fourth time Balaam opened his mouth, he prophesied: "A Star shall come out of Jacob; a Scepter shall rise out of Israel" (v. 17). In a trance, this unbelieving follower of witchcraft saw a vision of God and prophesied the word of God.

Even today, God can and does turn unbelieving occult followers into preachers of His gospel. A teenager once stood in our service and testified of Christ's intervention in her life. She and her friends had become deeply involved in Wicca, or supposed "white" magic. She had become dissatisfied with it and began to experiment with more blatant occult practices. Then she found herself gripped by something she could no longer control, and drug and alcohol abuse added to her problems.

Someone put this tormented young lady in contact with our deliverance counseling ministry. In a powerful encounter with God, she was gloriously saved and set free. She now gives her testimony to warn others of the dangers of playing around with the lure of power Satan uses to entangle souls.

Giver of Rest—Today!

It is easy to look at Biblical examples and believe God visited great spiritual leaders with seasons of rest, but then we doubt His attention to our present lives. This is a mistake. What God did then, He still does today.

Recent history reveals examples of those who discovered the rest and peace of God. Jonathan Edwards, the main instrument and theologian of the Great Awakening in the 1700s, not only witnessed the supernatural touch of God on his audiences, but he also saw his wife, Sarah, transformed after a visitation of God.

For a month in 1742, Sarah experienced an intense God-encounter, during which she had numerous fainting spells and was put to bed many times. She wrote that during these episodes, she swam in the light of Christ's love and that a "constant stream of sweet light" flowed between her and her Savior. Then as quickly as the episodes had begun, they ceased. After this experience, Sarah was even more a gracious, patient and loving wife and mother than before. She stopped straining to please God and lived her life in God's grace.

In these days of "latter rain revival," God is doing what He did in the Book of Acts. He wants His children to be world-changers, and longs to reach out to them with a visitation that will enable them to overcome fatigue and weariness. As we seek God's face, spend time in worship before Him, and open our hearts to His supernatural touch, we can know Him in the power of His resurrection.

Time-Out for the Weary

What does God do when He visits you with rest? God does exactly what He wants to do. His ways are not our ways, but we know that He does "all things well" (Mark 7:37). He may perform surgery, heal your body, send a prophecy, give you a promise, speak a word through you, send an angel, instruct, correct, deliver you, or call you to a new ministry. When God communicates from the Spirit of God into the spirit of man, He can bypass your mind, your will, your emotions, your thoughts, and your carnal desires and limitations.

If you are a mother, you may be familiar with the term *time-out*. Little children are often placed in a corner or chair in order to think about what they have done or failed to do. They are isolated from a group to calm their busy little bodies.

In the same way, we may need a time-out from our

busyness. Our heavenly Coach may choose to take us out of the game temporarily. He may pull us aside to say a word of praise for a job well done. Our Coach may need to say, "Come away and rest awhile!" He may even have a new play or assignment for us, or He may change the game plan altogether. The Father may sense that we are hurting and need time for healing. Whatever the reason for a time out with your heavenly Coach—listen to Him and trust Him, because it will always be for your good.

- ☞ You will gain rest as you reflect on God's work and provision in your life.

- ☞ You will praise Him and thank Him for every problem He solves and every provision He gives.

- ☞ You will worship Him in spirit and in truth.

- ☞ You will find rest when you remind God of your hurts and needs in prayer.

In doing this, you will be released from your cares, because Scripture teaches us to cast our cares on Him, because He cares for us (1 Peter 5:7). When you repent of your sin, you will find rest. The weight of sin so easily besets us, but "if we confess our sins, He is faithful and just to forgive us our sins and cleanse us from all unrighteousness" (1 John 1:9). Isn't it wonderful that God remembers our sins no more (Jeremiah 31:34; Hebrews 8:12; 10:17)? He removes our sins as far as the east is from the west (Psalm 103:12).

Rest comes as God removes all obstacles from you. The Book of Hebrews teaches that God rewards those who diligently seek Him (11:6), and James states, "Draw near to God and He will draw near to you" (4:8). Are you like Tommy Tenney says, a "God chaser"? Are you seeking Him with your whole heart?

You don't have to be a guest to use a room for rest. Find that secret place of the Most High and receive His strength by spending time with God. Isaiah 28:11, 12 states, "For with stammering lips and another tongue He will speak to His people, to whom He said, 'This is the rest with which you may cause the weary to rest' and, 'This is the refreshing.' "

Review Questions

1. List times when rest seems to elude you.

2. List three ways you can have rest with God.

3. Were you ever "slain in the Spirit"?

4. Look at the scriptures below recounting events of "resting in the Lord" and write in who was the recipient of the supernatural rest:

Scripture	Reason for the Experience	Individuals
Genesis 2:21	Surgery	
Genesis 15:12	Prophecy/ Blessing	
Numbers 24:4, 16	Unbeliever/ Blessing	
Ezekiel 1:28	Appearance	
Ezekiel 2:2	New Assignment	
Ezekiel 3:23	Vision/Prophecy	
Ezekiel 8:3	Abominations	

Scripture	Reason for the Experience	Individuals
Ezekiel 37:1	Prophecy/ Captivity	
Daniel 37:1	Prophecy/End Times	
Matthew 17:1-6	Show God's glory	
Matthew 28:4	Presence of God's power	
John 18:1-6	Power of Jesus' words	
Acts 9:4, 5	Deliverance/ Warning	
Acts 10:10-17	Receiving a new ministry	
Revelation 1:1, 10, 17	Prophecy/Vision	

5. Can you name examples from history of this "resting in the Lord"?

"Search me, O God, and know my heart: try me, and know my thoughts: And see if there be any wicked way in me, and lead me in the way everlasting" (Psalm 139:23, 24, KJV).

9

The Attic of Secret Sin

*I*magine that your house is for sale. The realtor calls and a prospective buyer wants to see your home in 10 minutes. Everything is in a state of chaos. Where do you hide everything in an emergency? Do you fill the clothes dryer, the car, the closet, the basement, the freezer or the outside storage building? Of course, the ideal place is a less-traveled area, like an attic.

Forty years ago, my parents had the most beautiful purple bedroom. It was remodeled with one long wall full of built-in extras and multiple mirrors flanking the vanity. All this was behind louvered doors. Everyone who visited our home wanted to see the master bedroom, because it was so ornate and stylish. I remember on one occasion when Mom gave me the glance that communicated the message, "Make the bed and straighten the room before I bring the company in." I did just that, but I had no idea where to put the clothes and incidentals that cluttered the room, so I threw everything on the vanity behind the louvered doors. That proved to be a temporary and unsatisfactory solution. Hiding things is no easy task.

When my children were small, I would "store" many of their toys for a few months so their rooms were uncluttered. After awhile, I would bring out their "new" toys, and they would eagerly play with them.

What Do You Hide?

Somehow we think the things we hide are not visible to others. It is in our nature to hide our shortcomings to others. In 1 Samuel 15, God told King Saul to utterly destroy their enemy, the Amalekites. God's orders were clear: Decimate everything, including women, children, men, buildings, oxen, sheep and possessions. Leave nothing.

Saul pretended to obey God's instructions. However, he kept the Amalekite king alive, and all the choice live-stock and possessions. He tried to hide these valuables from God and the prophet Samuel. Later, he claimed that the livestock would be sacrificed to God, but he proba-bly intended to put them in his own backyard.

In verse 14 Samuel said, "What then is this bleating of the sheep in my ears, and the lowing of the oxen which I hear?" But Saul kept denying that he had hidden any-thing from God. Have you ever tried to hide anything?

Remember playing hide-and-seek when you were a child? It is now a game I love to play with my grandsons. My first grandson, Ethan, would hide behind the open plantation shutters, peeking at me through the slats. I would pretend I couldn't find him, and then he would jump from the hiding place, laughing loudly. He always thought that he had fooled me.

When my daughter Heather was a preschooler, she loved sweets. I would look at her and ask, "Heather, have you been eating candy?" She would say, "No, Mommy," but I could see the telltale signs all over her little angelic face. I am sure that is what God sees when we try to hide things from Him. God knew Saul was hiding things from Him, and Samuel knew Saul was hiding things from God. Saul did not know the consequences of his sin would be great.

Storing Treasures or Trash?

The attic is a room of your heart where you store things. Some of those things are pleasant—lessons learned, memories and happy times. Other things in your attic are things you want out of your sight but don't necessarily want to destroy. Some of those things are unhealthy things.

Before I married, it was the custom for every girl to have a hope chest, or cedar chest, to fill with items needed for the marriage. Over the years, my own cedar chest has become a treasure trove of memories. I have found love notes from middle school, pictures, cards, gifts, napkins, football banners, pressed corsages, the topper off my wedding cake, a cap and tassel from one of my graduations, and baby shoes from one of my girls (now grown with children of their own). I found a very unflattering picture of my husband and me at the county fair. Included among the treasures was a picture of my fifth-grade class and Ron's stack of report cards from elementary school.

Along with present memories, however, we stash those secrets that we want no one to discover in our hidden attic. In the Shakespearian play *Macbeth*, the lead character was hiding a bloody secret. For a long time, no one knew he had murdered King Duncan to gain access to the throne. No one knew he had killed his best friend in order to keep the throne. During the course of the play, it became more difficult to hide his deeds. When he murdered the entire family of the nobleman Macduff, the whole country discovered all the awful secrets the madman Macbeth had tried to hide.

Secret sins are not easy to keep hidden. Psalm 69:5 states, "O God . . . my sins are not hidden from You."

Secret sins are not easy to keep hidden. Psalm 69:5 states, "O God, You know my foolishness; and my sins are not hidden from You." And in 1 Corinthians 4:5 we read, "The Lord comes, who will both bring to light the hidden things of darkness and reveal the counsels of the hearts."

If you are hiding secret sins, like adultery, illicit involvement or unholy flirtations, confess and repent before God. He will forgive you of your sins and allow you to start over.

A Box of Secrets

Women hide many things, but their weight is one thing that is next to impossible to hide. Perhaps you are hiding an eating disorder. Disorders associated with self-image plague teenage girls. Bulimia (binging and purging) and anorexia have become quite commonplace with the unnatural standards portrayed by models and actresses.

I remember the death of the young pop singer Karen Carpenter in the '70s. Her heart finally gave out after suffering from anorexia for years. Thousands of young girls pay a huge price for their obsession to be thin.

Perhaps your secret in the attic is a broken heart, from a broken engagement or a failed marriage. Depression overwhelms you as you look at wedding rings you no longer wear. Depression is something many women hide in their attics. Perhaps you suffered a broken heart, and loneliness overwhelms you. You trusted someone who failed you. You may have hung on to a sense of worthlessness or defeat, storing them in a box in your heart's attic. Although not visible to anyone else, these feelings haunt you with a sense of loss, failure and defeat. Why can't you rid yourself of the trinkets that continue to cause pain?

Many women hold on to baggage from their childhood. It may be a parent's divorce, a suicide or alcoholism in the family. Too many women have suffered physical, emotional or sexual abuse with memories they have revealed to no one.

You can be free of that debilitating memory. You can learn to trust again when you put your trust in Jesus Christ, who will "never leave you nor forsake you" (Hebrews 13:5).

Tools of Judgment

It is so damaging to have unwritten standards by which we measure those around us. If people fail us one time, then we write them off as friends. If they fail us a second time, we extend the tape measure for an even harsher measurement.

Just as we use a tape measure to judge another's actions, we use a sledgehammer to beat ourselves up emotionally.

Matthew 7:2 records, "For with what judgment you judge, you will be judged; and with the measure you use, it will be measured back to you." Matthew 6:14 reminds us, "For if you forgive men their trespasses, your heavenly Father will also forgive you." Verse 15 is most important: "But if you do not forgive men their trespasses, neither will your Father forgive your trespasses."

Throw away the tape measure and stop judging others. Leave all of that in God's hands.

Just as we use a tape measure to judge another's actions, we use a sledgehammer to beat ourselves up emotionally. We are often our own worst enemy, harboring negative thinking, insecurities and self-deprivation. This self-condemnation and self-criticism is a detriment for successful living. Romans 8:1 states, "There is therefore now no condemnation to those who are in Christ Jesus, who do not walk according to the flesh, but according to the Spirit." If your memory of that sin keeps defeating you, reject the memory. Know that these thoughts are not conviction—they are suggestions of the Enemy to discredit or discourage you.

Two more things we hide in the dark recesses of our attic are the viruses of jealousy and envy. *Jealousy* occurs when we have all we really need in life, yet we still want what others have. Jealousy is also the fear that something we possess will be taken from us. Some people are jealous of their possessions; others are jealous of people. Often jealousy shows its head in anxiety that you may lose your mate to someone else—someone who may seem more suitable, capable or beautiful than you are.

Envy, on the other hand, is to desire something someone else possesses. The Ten Commandments teach us, "Thou shalt not covet thy neighbor's house . . . servant . . . ox . . . donkey . . . land . . . or anything that belongs to your neighbor."

Benjamin Franklin said, "It is the eyes of other people that ruin us. If all but myself were blind, I would neither have a fine house nor fine furniture." Envy reared its head in the trial of Jesus. Matthew 27:18 records that Pilate turned Jesus over to be crucified although he knew "they had handed Him over because of envy."

Jealousy begins when we start comparing our cars, houses and paychecks with one another. Before long, you begin to think others are better than you because of their possessions. This leads to low self-esteem—a by-product of jealousy.

Shakespeare said that jealousy is a "poison more deadly than a mad dog's tooth" and is a "green-eyed monster."

John Dryden called it the "jaundice of the soul." Shakespeare also wrote the tragedy *Othello,* about the love and marriage of a Moor general in a Venetian army who was married to a beautiful noblewoman. Because of envy, hate and racism, Iago, a trusted officer, plotted to lie and convince General Othello that his wife was in love with a Lieutenant Cassio. The play ends with Othello murdering his innocent wife. Blinded by jealousy, he killed the person who was most precious to him.

Criticism is the outward sign of inner jealousy. When we are successful, we believe it is all because of ability and talent. But when we fail, we believe it is only due to circumstances beyond our control. Of course, we are quick to say, "It is only due to luck," when other people succeed. These attitudes indicate a root of jealousy.

There is a story of two shopkeepers who were bitter rivals. Since their stores were directly across the street from each other, they could track each other's customer flow. When one had a successful sale, he would smile gloatingly across the street to his rival.

One night, an angel appeared to one of the shopkeepers in a dream and said, "You can have one wish for anything you desire; the catch is that your competitor will receive twice as much of whatever you request. You can be rich, but he will be richer. You can live healthy, but he will be healthier and live longer. What do you desire?"

The shopkeeper thought about it and then said, "Here is my request: make me blind in one eye!" (Thomas Lindberg, *sermonillustrations.com*)

If it is easier for you to weep with those who weep than to rejoice with those who rejoice, you may have a root of jealousy in your attic. Jealousy robs you of your peace with God, because it causes you to be judgmental and have resentful attitudes. Proverbs 14:30 warns, "A sound heart is life to the body, but envy is rottenness to the bones."

Holy Housecleaning

If you have accepted Christ as your Lord and Savior, you are free from the devil's power through the crucifixion of Christ and His resurrection. Your victory and freedom were purchased on Calvary. But you must walk in that freedom by taking a stand against the suggestions of the Enemy concerning your life. We do this by praying the truth of God's Word, renouncing all evil in our lives. Declare out loud your faith and belief in God's Word and in His Son.

You gain freedom from the hidden secrets of your heart when you . . .

♥ Confess your sins

♥ Forgive others who have hurt you

♥ Renounce all evil

♥ Turn from your jealous ways.

Do not hang onto the chains in your attic. How do you turn over the chains of hurt to Christ? First, take care of the issues in the attic one at a time. In prayer, go to God in confession and repentance. Then forgive others for their mistreatment of you.

Renounce all sin that overwhelms you and turn away from it, with promises from God's Word.

And there is no creature hidden from His sight, but all things are naked and open to the eyes of Him to whom we must give account. Seeing then that we have a great High Priest who has passed through the heavens, Jesus the Son of God, let us hold fast our confession. For we do not have a High Priest who cannot sympathize with our weaknesses, but was in all points tempted as we are, yet without sin. Let us therefore come boldly to the throne of grace, that we may obtain mercy and find grace to help in time of need (Hebrews 4:13-16).

Jesus died on the cross so we could have healing over these hurtful things. All things in our lives can become new with Him, and we can find mercy in our time of need. God will replace the secret hurts with good things: power, love and a sound mind.

What has harassed you from the attic of secrets?

- If it is food—substitute the Bread of Life who is Jesus.

- If it is the pain of the past—remember you are a new creation in Christ.

- If it is unforgiveness—confess, repent and forgive.

- If it is sin or shame—renounce the hidden things of shame (2 Corinthians 4:2).

- If it is a critical spirit—ask in prayer for God to "renew a right spirit within [you]." (Psalm 51:10, KJV).

- If it is depression—put on a garment of praise.

Is Your Attic in Charge?

It all comes down to control. Are the hidden sins of your past controlling you? Escape from living in the shadows by letting God fill your life, repair the damaged places and wipe away your tears. Strengthen your heart and salvage your home by destroying the junk in your attic.

Review Questions

1. In 1 Samuel 15, what was the source of King Saul's guilt?

2. Do you remember a time when a young child tried to hide something from you?

3. Where do you hide things in your home? Do you keep an inventory of your storage, or would there be hidden surprises there?

4. List some of the treasures you keep in a box of memories or a cedar chest.

5. Consider the attic of your heart—what is in your box of hidden secrets?

6. How do each of these passages encourage us to open our hearts and reveal our secrets to a holy God?

   Hebrews 4:12-16

   Isaiah 61

   Deuteronomy 29:29

Psalm 27:5, 6

Matthew 6:6

1 Peter 3:4

Psalm 44:21

Psalm 9:5

Psalm 119:11

Psalm 91:1

2 Corinthians 4:2

Matthew 22:37-40

"What saves a man is to take a step.
Then another step."
—C.S. Lewis

10

The Hallway of Transition

Many rooms in my house bring me comfort. In the bedroom, I have everything I need—I can sleep, rest, read, eat, watch television and do my nails. Another comfort zone in my home is the kitchen. We congregate there for meals, for creative cooking and for conversations at the table. I can talk on the phone and still get my chores done in the kitchen.

However, there is one room in my house where I am most uncomfortable. This is the hallway.

The hallway is a long, dark corridor. You would probably never sit and relax in a hallway, because there is generally no furniture. No windows open in the hallway to bring in the sunshine or gentle breezes. The doors along the hallway usually are closed, occasionally locked. It is an ominous and foreboding place to be.

The hallway is not really a room at all; it is only a passageway from one place to another—a transition. While change and new direction can make transition a "hall of fame," unfortunately they can also become places of shame. Transitions may prompt us to unleash our fury and anger in times of failure. In the hallway, we often want to make excuses and blame God, which leads to bitterness.

Your Father, who knows when a sparrow falls to the ground, knows when you fall also! God is with you in the dark, transitional times in your life.

Perhaps as you read this, you are in a state of discontent. You may even be miserable in your Christian faith because you have expectations and promises from God that have not become a reality. You have read the Scripture, prayed and believed that God will do a specific thing for you personally or for your family, but it just has not happened. Your hopes, dreams and promises are unfulfilled.

Woman of God, remember, you are not alone! Your Father, who knows when a sparrow falls to the ground, knows when you fall also! God is with you in the dark, transitional times of your life. Scripture tells us that He will never leave us nor forsake us (Hebrews 13:5). Whatever you are enduring in the hallway, just know that events and circumstances in your life *will not* and *cannot* cancel the promises of God for you.

You Have Purpose

God designed you with purpose and intent. His goals for you are good. If God, who created the entire universe, the galaxies and everything on earth, can keep His world in balance and functioning, He can keep you. If God can keep the earth revolving, the seasons in balance, the flowers blooming, the animals reproducing and the harvest growing, He can surely see you safely through the difficult hallways of change. Psalm 139 confirms this:

> For You formed my inward parts; You covered me in my mother's womb. I will praise You, for I am fearfully and wonderfully made. . . . How precious also are Your thoughts to me, O God! How great is the sum of them! If I should count them, they would be more in number than the sand (v. 13, 14, 17, 18).

The next time you walk on the beach and the sand collects between your toes, remember that every grain of sand represents a thought God has toward you! You have a unique purpose that only you can complete. Don't lose heart, for the events of your life were no accident. God knows what you have been experiencing.

Everything you have been through has a purpose from God. Every friend you have had, every neighborhood you have lived in, has had a purpose. Every job you have ever held, and every job you have ever lost had a purpose for you. God never abdicated His control. Everything has a purpose under heaven. Proverbs 4:18 says, "The path of the just is like the shining sun that shines even brighter unto the perfect day."

The longer you serve the Lord, the brighter your life can shine to others. You may ask, "Well, why am I in the middle of so many problems then?" or "I wish God would explain to me why this has happened!"

A Dark Hallway for Job

In the Old Testament, the richest man in the East was a man named Job. He had the perfect life. Satan came to God and said, "If You remove all Job's riches, Job will curse You to Your face" (see Job 1:11). So God allowed Satan to test him. In a single day, Job lost all 10 of his children in death. He lost all his herds, camels, flocks, home and lands. Yet, he did not curse God, but exclaimed, "Naked I came from my mother's womb, and naked I shall return there. . . . Blessed be the name of the Lord" (v. 21).

Next, Satan received permission to attack Job's health. Scripture tells us Job was stricken with horrible sores. He had gone from riches and happiness to poverty and illness. I would say that Job was in a difficult hallway of transition.

However, the end of the hallway would come for Job. When the test was over, God restored everything back to him. Job was given back double all that he had lost.

Often we hear the story of Job and forget an important fact: God *never* explained to Job why he went through that difficult period of his life. God does not have to explain anything to us. We may never know the answers to our questions until we get to heaven.

Another Old Testament character who went through a time of transition was Noah. Because Noah was a righteous man, God decided to spare him from the destruction of the world. Noah built an ark, as directed by God. He further obeyed Him by preaching repentance to the crowds. When the Flood came, Noah and seven other family members escaped God's judgment.

Safely in the ark, they knew they were protected, yet look at how long those eight people were on that boat. According to Genesis 7:11, 12 and 8:13, 14, Noah and his family were on the ark for one year and 10 days. Can you imagine the extent of cabin fever? Leaving behind their old life, they knew a new future lay ahead, but they had not yet received a promise of what it would entail. Surely Noah felt uncertain of how to start over. He must have had questions about the outcome of it all. Was he discouraged because he didn't see the sun for over a year? More than once, Noah probably said, "How much longer, Lord, will I have to clean up after these elephants?" Did anyone get seasick? Was the stench of that situation overwhelming?

The hallway of transition between the old life and the new life had to be difficult. All Noah had was the assurance that God had provided the ark as a means to obtain His purpose, which was to start over and repopulate the earth. Events and circumstances did not, and cannot, cancel the promises of God.

Twenty-four years ago, when we moved to Tennessee from Alabama, we had a very difficult time financially. Central Baptist was a small and struggling church that could barely pay for moving our family. They certainly couldn't help us with house payments until our home in Alabama sold. For 10 months, we had to make two house payments.

On paper, that was impossible. We were in a hallway of transition. One ministry was over; the next ministry had not fully begun. But God provided during the transition. Even though money was tight, every month extra money simply showed up so we could make two house payments. When our home in Alabama finally sold, we no longer had that extra money. Our faith had grown tremendously.

At the End of the Hall

In the hallways of your life, God is putting you in situations where your faith must operate fully. Don't curse the hallways of your life. Just remember these are paths to get you from your past to your future. Don't be tempted to curse your job, situations, salary, church, town, family or friends. You are continually on your way *through* this passageway.

While speaking to our church recently, John Kilpatrick gave us a powerful illustration. Holding a large key, he explained that the circumstances of your life are like the grooves and cutting teeth on a key. As you are on your way through the hallway, the Holy Spirit will use situations to cut notches and grooves in your key, preparing you for the moment you arrive at the locked door at the end of the hallway.

It's during the dark, trying times in your life that you learn compassion, love and understanding. You will be able to use the key of your past to help others in the future. Your heartaches prepare you to help others.

You Can Find Peace

The hallway can be a place of chaos. You may think that this season of your life will never end. You may have lack and want. You may be struggling with extra bills and difficulties. You may be waiting in the dark hallway praying for erring children who won't live right and grow up. Health problems, addictions or a nervous breakdown may cause you to lose hope. God has the power to speak to the chaos in your life, and He will. Just as He spoke the world into existence with a simple word, He can speak peace that passes understanding. You may be struggling in the hallway of divorce. You are not truly married for there is no man at your home or father to your children. Yet, you are not technically free since the divorce is not final. You may be angry and confused. This upset in your life brings with it upheaval and devastation. You may be bitter and hardened, but take your needs to the Lord. During the dark of the hallway, you can find Him to be your anchor and strong tower. God will teach you to depend on Him. You will learn to pray and get hold of God. Speak to your soul with scriptures such as Psalm 42:5:

> Why are you cast down, O my soul? And why are you disquieted within me? Hope in God, for I shall yet praise Him for the help of His countenance.

Even in the difficult hallways, God will give the "peace of God, which surpasses all understanding, [and] will guard your hearts and minds through Christ Jesus" (Philippians 4:7).

An Old Testament example of a man who had peace in the hallway was Caleb. In Joshua 14:7-15, we read where Caleb and Joshua were the only spies who believed God would give them victory over the Canaanites. The others were cowards. Caleb asked for and was promised the mountain of Hebron as his own inheritance. But because of Israel's sin, they would not enter the Promised Land for another 40 years.

At 85 years old, Caleb finally entered the land of "milk and honey" and received his mountain. He patiently waited through a 45-year hallway of transition before he saw the promises of God fulfilled.

Power From Above

Have you been in the transition a long time? God uses all the junk in your life to remind you of His vast love and supernatural intervention. God alone changes us, molds us and refines us for the unlocked door of our future. Romans 8:28 says, "All things work together for good to those who love God, to those who are the called according to His purpose."

> *God alone changes us, molds us and refines us for the unlocked door of our future.*

Jonah was a prophet in the Old Testament who knew firsthand the consequences of running away from God's assignment. God told Jonah to go east to Nineveh, but Jonah fled west to Tarshish. Because of his disobedience, Jonah was thrown overboard in the middle of the night into a raging, threatening thunderstorm. God prepared for Jonah a three-day transition experience in the belly of a great fish. Jonah said of that experience: "I cried to the

Lord because of my affliction, and He answered me. Out of the belly of Sheol I cried, and You heard my voice" (Jonah 2:2, 3; see also vv. 4-7).

Jonah ended up sloshing around in the gastrointestinal juices of a great fish's stomach. I imagine that was a rough ride that made him seasick and nauseous. Seaweed probably covered his body. Continual billows of water passed over him; undigested sea life probably surrounded him, and the stench must have been abhorrent! The throat of the fish closed him in like bars in a prison. Those three days must have seemed like a lifetime.

Only after Jonah prayed, accepted the assignment, renewed his vow and thanked God for his deliverance did the fish spit Jonah out on the shore. Jonah was out of the hallway of transition and on to pursue the purpose for which God had called him.

He preached with the power of God and saw a great repentance across the land. God's heart was moved for mercy and the nation was spared His judgment. Zechariah 4:6 reminds us, "'Not by might nor by power, but by My Spirit' says the Lord of hosts."

My friend Mae tells as part of her testimony that she felt as if she was in the hallway of transition most of her life. Her alcoholic father rarely worked, and when he did, he used his payday for alcohol. Her family lived in a four-room house above a bar. The house had no heat or air. She remembers times when they had no food for three days. She had to hide from her physically abusive brother, because her mother instructed her to stay out of his way and anything he did was her fault.

She didn't have a good education, and people said she

wouldn't amount to much. However, a neighbor took her to church and Mae loved it. She received a Bible, which she read behind closed doors at night. Through reading that Bible she heard God say deep within her, "Mae, I believe in you."

She married a fine Christian man and both of them have been leaders in our church for 25 years. As an activities director for a nursing facility, my friend shows Christ's love and compassion daily. Two years ago, a Christian director came to her facility. Each day in Bible study, the director would announce to all the workers, "I believe in you." She even provided them with pins with that statement on them.

Striding confidently through her hallway of transition, my friend Mae never lost faith. Competing against 1,600 applicants, her organization recently awarded her the title of National Activities Director for the United States. She will serve on a committee in Washington to speak on behalf of the elderly. God prepared this promotion at the end of her hallway.

Acts 1:8 states, "But you shall receive power when the Holy Spirit has come upon you; and you shall be witnesses."

If you have thought about giving up or going back, don't. If you have blamed God, stop. If you have been bitter about circumstances, forgive. There is hope in the Lord Jesus Christ. Our Lord can take you through your dark hallway and turn it into a bridge to the future. You will be numbered with the friends of God.

Review Questions

1. What hopes, dreams and promises are unfulfilled in your life?

2. You have a purpose in God from Creation. Read Psalm 139 and Proverbs 4:18, and list some of the things God thinks of you as His child.

3. Remember something negative from your past that God has now used in a positive way to help you and others.

4. Review the story of Job. Did God ever explain to Job why he went through so much tragedy?

5. Why do you think the hallway of transition is such a difficult place to be?

6. Explain how Noah and his family were in transition while on the ark. Genesis 7 and 8 indicate they were there for more than a year. What happens when life is put on hold for a year?

7. God's Word gives comfort in transition. Look up the following scriptures, and tell why each can encourage you during difficulty: Psalm 42:5; Philippians 1:6.

8. Jonah underwent a dramatic three-day transition that changed his life and the lives of a whole nation of people. How were they changed?

9. List positive lessons you learned in difficult transitions in your life. How did God use those times to prepare you for where you are now?

"Beloved, I pray that you may prosper
in all things and be in health,
just as your soul prospers."
(3 John 2).

11

The Workout Room of Health

The longer a woman lives, the more attention she feels she must give to health and beauty aids. The feminine mystique covets the balance of discipline, charm, style, health and unique purpose. Women today want to do anything, try anything and buy anything that will enhance health and retain youthful beauty and vigor.

Women want it all—beauty, brains and brawn—yes, even muscular strength. Recently, Sporting Goods Manufacturing Association (SGMA), a global trade association of manufacturers and marketers in the sporting industry, reported that Americans spent over $11 billion on gym memberships in a year. Experts tell us which exercise regimen is the best, which vitamins or dietary supplements are the most effective, and which diet will get the biggest results. In spite of the expert advice, we still struggle to get the help we so much desire.

A Natural Facelift
Ecclesiastes 8:1 states, "Wisdom brightens a person's

face and changes its hard appearance" (*NIV*). What a revolutionary idea, that wisdom softens a face that otherwise is chiseled by time and circumstances. As women of faith, we must realize that general health and beauty affect the whole person. Proverbs 3:7, 8 states, "Fear the Lord and shun evil. This will bring health to your body and nourishment to your bones" (*NIV*).

> *Maintaining good health depends on the "whole" person. . . . God is the author of the whole-man approach.*

Maintaining good health depends on the "whole" person. We hear a lot about the wholeness approach in many areas today, such as the whole language approach in education. But God is the author of the whole-man approach. He made us to operate best in perfect balance, and if one part is out of line, every part suffers. We are a spirit, we live in a body, and we have a mind. All three are closely connected. Keeping these in balance and maintaining wellness requires a constant effort on our part.

The apostle Paul said in 1 Corinthians 6:19, 20, "Do you not know that your body is the temple of the Holy Spirit who is in you, whom you have from God, and you are not your own? For you were bought at a price; therefore glorify God in your body and in your spirit, which are God's."

The Disciplined Woman

God created all of us to be goal-oriented and have

tenacity. What are your goals and motives? We're told that whatever screams the loudest is usually what gets our attention. The older I get, I find that I need more discipline in order to maintain a balanced diet and exercise program.

A few years ago, my daughter, a girlfriend and I signed up for a monthlong exercise "boot camp." Since I knew and trusted the personal trainer, I was proud that I had taken the first steps to fitness and just knew the pounds would come slipping off. I could not have been more wrong.

For four nights a week all that month, my 50-year-old body struggled to keep up with a class full of cross-country skiers, marathon runners, triathlon competitors and weight lifters half my age! Shinsplints, sore muscles, discouragement and sheer agony were always present. I actually thought I might die.

I did feel a sense of pride and amazement that I went from five push-ups the first night to 35 on the last night. However, I was disheartened to find that at the end of the month, I had gained five pounds. I was assured that it was due to muscle gain in the place where fat used to live. It was a month I will truly never forget.

Are you struggling with issues of weight? Maybe the motive for losing the 10 (or 50) pounds is a high school reunion, your child's upcoming marriage, a cruise to the Caribbean or a special anniversary celebration. Or your motive may be more serious—you may be attempting a lifestyle change for health reasons. Careful diet and exercise practices may be required because of the threats of type II diabetes, high blood pressure, high cholesterol or osteoarthritis.

Whatever the motive for losing the weight, our goal should be more than simply to change the outward appearance. Remember that Proverbs 31:30 states, "Charm is deceitful and beauty is passing." So the larger goal should not be just a magic number on the scales, but a healthy lifestyle change.

The ultimate motivation for losing weight or changing our lifestyles is so that our lives honor God.

A healthier lifestyle involves discipline, moderation, motivation and self-control. First Corinthians 9:24 tells us, "Do you not know that in a race all the runners run, but only one gets the prize? Run in such a way as to get the prize" (*NIV*). The apostle Paul continues in verses 26 and 27, "I do not run like a man running aimlessly; I do not fight like a man beating the air. No, I beat my body and make it my slave so that after I have preached to others, I myself will not be disqualified for the prize" (*NIV*). In these verses and others, Paul compares the Christian life to an athletic competition.

As we become more spiritually mature, we should curb blatant desires to overeat or eat unhealthy foods. With the help of the Holy Spirit, along with discipline and exercise, we can control these urges. I admit I don't always succeed. To me, nothing is more disheartening than to exercise and eat right for a week or two, only to have a day when the craving for ice cream, donuts or supersized fast food overcomes me. When that happens, we simply must pick up where we left off and begin again.

The ultimate motivation for losing weight or changing our lifestyles is so that our lives honor God. If our bodies are temples of the Holy Spirit, then taking care of our bodies will honor our Creator God. This is not vanity or self-centeredness, but it is something we do out of love for our Father.

The Healthy Woman

According to Don Colbert, M.D., 85 percent of all deaths are related to a toxic lifestyle that may result in heart disease, cancer, stroke, diabetes or obesity. He further stated that a build-up of toxins can cause symptoms of fatigue, memory loss, premature aging, skin problems, arthritis, hormone imbalances, chronic fatigue, anxiety, emotional disorders, and more. In his book *Toxic Relief,* Colbert encourages the reader to cleanse the body of toxins caused by pollution, bacteria, mold, yeast, smoke, pesticides, fat, water, solvents, additives, processed food and other sources.

Your best starting point is to see your doctor for a complete physical. Many women dread making that appointment for an annual physical with their general doctor or OB/GYN, but it is important to take these steps for your health and well-being.

Take time to pamper yourself. Take care of your body with massages, facials, skin care products, such as skin creams, oils and lotions. Take supplements if you need them. Every stage of a woman's life has different requirements as she changes from childhood to menstruation, to PMS, to perimenopause, menopause, to postmenopause. Health books are on the best-seller list all the time. Doctors are on television all the time with the latest in health news, but simply knowing the information is not enough. We must actually act on the information. Having vitamins in our home is not enough. We must take them consistently.

Romans 7:15-25 tells how the apostle Paul struggled with these same issues. He basically said, "The things I hate, I do, and the things I want to do are the things I don't do." He even called himself a "wretched man" (v. 24). He was exhausted from trying to change himself. That is specifically why we need to take one day at a time and pray for God's help with each health issue.

Power in Numbers

I've discovered that having outside support is key to success when you are attempting a lifestyle change. Find a friend to be an accountability partner who will tell you the truth. Find someone who, like you, wants to be all God has purposed her to be. Change is easier if we don't have to go it alone. A partner will ask the difficult questions. Share your goals. Get connected with those people who need what you need and are serious about change.

Encourage yourself with Biblical patterns for change and success stories from the Bible. Jesus said in John 10:10, "I have come that they may have life, and that they may have it more abundantly."

The Charming Woman

History recorded that on December 11, 1936, King Edward VIII of England gave up his throne to marry American divorcée Wallis Simpson. In a worldwide radio broadcast Edward said, "I have found it impossible to carry the heavy burden of responsibility and to discharge my duties as king, as I wish to do, without the help and support of the woman I love." This was the love story and scandal of the century. Why would a king give up his throne for a woman? She must have been both charming and mysterious.

To be a mysterious and charming woman, we must concentrate on the following:

～ Keep and enlarge another's interest.

～ Rise above challenges and obstacles.

～ Develop charm, mystique and beauty.

～ Acquire an inner confidence.

～ Display both poise and class.

～ Hold tight to self-esteem.

When I think of these qualities, I think of famous women like Jacqueline Kennedy Onassis, Nancy Reagan and Princess Diana. These women had incredible strength and character. They faced every obstacle and looked forward to the future. They were independent, individualistic and loved unconditionally.

A woman may have beauty but not a pretty face. Beauty is often reflected in the way we carry ourselves, with self-assured actions and style. Maturity—coupled with wisdom, appearance and super attitude—makes a woman unique and charming.

A woman of mystery develops her own style, finding what works for her. You don't need a big bank account or closets filled with clothes to improve your appearance or self-esteem. If you really do feel you don't have a grasp of good style and tastes, ask a friend to help you. A professional can determine a palette of colors for your skin tone, and a facial will help you decide on the right makeup. A woman of charm has an inner beauty that comes from taking care of her body, mind and spirit. This beautiful poem by Audrey Hepburn was read at her funeral.

You don't need a big bank account or closets filled with clothes to improve your appearance or self-esteem.

For attractive lips, speak words of kindness.
For lovely eyes, seek out the good in people.
For a slim figure, share your food with the
    hungry.
For beautiful hair, let a child run his/her fingers
    through it once a day.
For poise, walk with the knowledge that you
    never walk alone.
People, even more than things, have to
    restored, renewed, revived, reclaimed, and
    redeemed; never throw anyone out.

Beauty is never shabby or sloppy. It creates energy, calms the spirit, and reduces tension, stress and anxiety. I personally believe a woman of charm has a thirst for knowledge that continues throughout her lifetime.

The Ageless Woman

I have a friend whose mother, widowed for 35 years, remarried at 80 years of age. She is an ageless, vibrant woman who is very much in love.

My friend called her mother one night. Having difficulty hearing her, she asked, "What is that loud music I hear?"

Her mother answered, "Oh, we are just dancing to 'Love Me Tender' by Elvis!" These newlyweds have been married several years, and they still love life and each other. Truly the end of their lives is the grand finale—worth waiting for!

A woman of charm loves herself, her body and her God. She possesses these characteristics:

꙳ She is filled with faith in God, who is her strength.

꙳ She loves life and savors each moment.

꙳ She is vital, enthusiastic and growing in the things of God.

However, a woman of charm is not perfect.

꙳ She knows she is vulnerable.

꙳ She has problems, but she admits her weaknesses.

꙳ She is not embarrassed by her problems.

ᵡ She rides the waves and is not crushed in the under-
tow.

In his book, *Woman, Thou Art Loosed,* T.D. Jakes
described the breaking of a new day:

> Like the initial sounds of an orchestra warming up for a
> concerto, the sea gulls cried and screeched out their
> opening solos. The wind watched, occasionally brush-
> ing past the palm trees spreading their leaves like the fan
> of a distinguished lady. Far to the east the sun crept up
> on stage as if it were trying to arrive without disturbing
> anyone. It peeked up over the ocean like the eye of a
> child around a corner as he stealthily plays peek-a-boo.

Later, he obeserves the sun as it begins its descent over
the horizon. "The grace of a closing day is far greater than
the uncertainty of morning," he said. "[And] the most
beautiful part of a woman's life is at the setting of the sun."

Oh, how we women want to believe that! The
Scripture teaches that the end of a thing is better than the
beginning. After reading that beautiful prose, I think of
my own mother, who turned 75 this year. I give her a
standing ovation for her charm, her strength, her steadfast
love and her faith in God. I am a grateful daughter who
has received the rewards of her labors and her dreams.

My mother is active in her church, she paints daily,
she walks on her treadmill and does water aerobics
weekly. Her eyesight is better than mine, and her insight,
wisdom and advice are always right on target.
Circumstances have chiseled away at her heart, and
tragedies have bruised her, but to me she is still very
regal. In the winter season of her life, she is peace,

warmth and strength for her husband, her children, grandchildren and great-grandchildren. My mother has always been courageous and comfortable with herself, and she is confident in us.

I have two daughters and one daughter-in-love who are in the springtime of their lives. They are mothers, filled with hope, desires and aspirations for the future. Their beauty, strength and youth seem dauntless. I have one infant granddaughter who in wide-eyed wonder will experience the wonderful journey just as the women before her.

Even though Dolly Parton said in *Steel Magnolias*, "Time marches on and sooner or later, you realize it is marching across your face," I have purposed to celebrate the changes of middle age with laughter, purpose, adaptation and grace. My mother, my daughters and my granddaughter stand with me—four generations of strong women. It is my prayer that our lives will be a symphony celebrating all the seasons of life.

As Robert Browning, the great poet, wrote so long ago:

Grow old along with me
The best is yet to be
The last of life, for which the first was made
Our times are in His hand
Who saith, "A whole I planned
Youth shows but half;
Trust God: see all, nor be afraid!"

Take one day at a time. Be a disciplined woman, a healthy woman, a charming woman and an ageless woman—and enjoy the journey!

Review Questions

1. Write out 1 Corinthians 6:19, 20 in your own words.

2. It takes spirit, mind and body for us to have balance. Relate the ways you struggle with balance in your life.

3. What are your immediate health needs? How are you taking care of those needs?

4. What should be your overall motivation for losing weight?

5. What forms of physical exercise do you do? How often do you exercise? Who can be your partner in exercise?

6. How is your body like a sporting competition in 1 Corinthians 9:24-27? Read 2 Timothy 4:7 and Galatians 2:2 and determine if you are honoring God in your body.

7. Do an inventory of your health status:

What vitamins do you need?

What foods should you eat?

What foods should you avoid?

Who can be your accountability partner?

8. Read Romans 7:15-25 and make a commitment to care for the body God has given you.

9. In what areas can you become a more disciplined woman? In what ways can you become a more charming woman? Do you need to adjust your attitude about growing older?

10. Consider your favorite woman—entertainer, mentor, friend or relative. How does her beauty transcend age and circumstances?

11. List the many attributes that make you a charming and ageless woman. (And don't be modest!)

Conclusion

$\mathcal{Y}$our dream life is attainable. If you have felt unsettled or pricked with the conviction of the issues covered as we toured each room of your heart, know that you can have a remodeled life. Review each issue that applies to you, and take it to God in prayer—He will allow you to start over.

Do you remember the "Etch a Sketch" toy we played with as children? It was simple to scribble any drawing on the surface, and with one swift shake, clean the whole slate again. When we pray, God can shake things up in our hearts, our attitudes and our habits. He can make our hearts clean again. He can teach us to pray and lift our loneliness.

When you become intimate with God, you can become close to others, especially your husband. God can give you wisdom for parenting and a love for hospitality to your own family and even strangers. God, through Jesus Christ, will destroy the hidden sins and give you a new beginning. He will restore your health and give you peace in the transitions of life. When you are hassled and feel that you cannot get it together, God will give you rest.

What women don't know *will* hurt them. You may think you are not better than your problems, but God is. If these issues in your life need changing or fixing, turn to God and He will give you wisdom. Proverbs 24:3 states, "Through wisdom a house is built and by understanding it is established; by knowledge the rooms are filled with all precious and pleasant riches."

It is my prayer that this book has introduced you to the truth about your life and the power of God to change your heart. I pray that an extraordinary relationship will begin between you and the God who loves you.

Dear heavenly Father:

I thank You for the gift of Your Son, Jesus Christ, to give us life to its fullest. I praise You, because You made each one of us unique. I invite Your presence and power to change my life. I thank You that I am Your child and part of Your family. By Your power I can experience freedom, victory and restoration.

I pray for each person who reads this book that You will give them the desires of their hearts—including a passion and devotion to the principles of Your Word, the Bible. May their hearts be renewed with laughter and joy. May they be strengthened—full of virtue, knowledge, self-control and godliness. May God guard their hearts and minds through Christ Jesus. May they allow the Master Builder (God) to continue His work in progress until we all reach eternity. May they be blessed in every way. Through Christ Jesus our Lord, Amen.

Bibliography

Anderson, Neil, and Dave Park. *The Bondage Breaker.* Eugene, OR: Harvest, 1993.

Bevere, John. *Breaking Intimidation.* Altamonte Springs, FL: Creation, 1997.

"Biblical Portrait of Marriage" video series by Bruce Wilkerson. Copyright © 1995 Walk Through the Bible Ministries Inc.

Colbert, Don, M.D. *Toxic Relief.* Lake Mary, FL: Siloam, 2001.

Dobson, Shirley, and Gloria Gaither. *Let's Make a Memory.* Waco, TX: Word, 1994.

"In the Meantime" audio sermon by John Kilpatrick presented Sept. 20, 2002, available at the *www.brownsville-revival.org* bookstore.

Jakes, T.D. *Woman, Thou Art Loosed: Healing the Wounds of the Past.* Shippensburg, PA: Destiny Image, 1994. 160-61.

Lush, Jean. *Emotional Phases of a Woman's Life.* Old Tappan, NJ: Fleming H. Revell, 1990.

MacDonald, James. *I Really Want to Change . . . So, Help Me God.* Chicago: Moody, 2000.

Maxwell, John. "Raising Kids in a Glass House" video series. From Leadership Growth Series, San Diego, CA.

McDowell, Josh and Dick Day. *How to Be a Hero to Your Kids.* Waco, TX: Word, 1993.

Phillips, Ron. *Awakened by the Spirit: Reclaiming the Forgotten Gift of God.* Nashville: Thomas Nelson, 1999.

Phillips, Ron and Paulette. *Song of Solomon: Invitation to Intimacy.* Cleveland, TN: Pathway, 2003.

Davis, Kara. "Staying Fit for the Right Reasons." *Spirit Led Woman.* (Strang Communications. April/May 2003) 58-62.

Zigler, Zig. *Raising Positive Kids in a Negative World.* Nashville: Thomas Nelson, 2002.